John Lyly's Sappho and Phao: A Retelling

David Bruce

Published by David Bruce, 2022.

This is a work of fiction. Similarities to real people, places, or events are entirely coincidental.

JOHN LYLY'S SAPPHO AND PHAO: A RETELLING

First edition. October 15, 2022.

Copyright © 2022 David Bruce.

ISBN: 979-8215890981

Written by David Bruce.

Table of Contents

CAST OF CHARACTERS..1

CHAPTER 1 | — 1.1 — 3

— 1.2 — 8

— 1.3 — 13

— 1.4 — 16

CHAPTER 2 | — 2.1 — 19

— 2.2 — 28

— 2.3 — 30

— 2.4 — 36

CHAPTER 3 | — 3.1 — 46

— 3.2 — 49

— 3.3 — 54

— 3.4 — 62

CHAPTER 4 | — 4.1 — 67

— 4.2 — 68

— 4.3 — 71

— 4.4 — 76

CHAPTER 5 | — 5.1 — 80

— 5.3 — 88

EPILOGUE 90

NOTES | — 1.1 — 91

— 1.1 — 93

— 3.4 — 94

— 3.4 — 95

— 3.4 — 96

— 4.4 — 97

— Entire Play — 98

APPENDIX A: FAIR USE 99

APPENDIX B: ABOUT THE AUTHOR 100

APPENDIX C: SOME BOOKS BY DAVID BRUCE........................101

Dedication

Dedicated to Carl Eugene Bruce and Josephine Saturday Bruce

My father, Carl Eugene Bruce, died on 24 October 2013. He used to work for Ohio Power, and at one time, his job was to shut off the electricity of people who had not paid their bills. He sometimes would find a home with an impoverished mother and some children. Instead of shutting off their electricity, he would tell the mother that she needed to pay her bill or soon her electricity would be shut off. He would write on a form that no one was home when he stopped by because if no one was home he did not have to shut off their electricity.

The best good deed that anyone ever did for my father occurred after a storm that knocked down many power lines. He and other linemen worked long hours and got wet and cold. Their feet were freezing because water got into their boots and soaked their socks. Fortunately, a kind woman gave my father and the other linemen dry socks to wear.

My mother, Josephine Saturday Bruce, died on 14 June 2003. She used to work at a store that sold clothing. One day, an impoverished mother with a baby clothed in rags walked into the store and started shoplifting in an interesting way: The mother took the rags off her baby and dressed the infant in new clothing. My mother knew that this mother could not afford to buy the clothing, but she helped the mother dress her baby and then she watched as the mother walked out of the store without paying.

My mother and my father both died at 7:40 p.m.

Cover Photograph for John Lyly's *Sappho and Phao*: A Retelling: DucHaiten
https://pixabay.com/illustrations/woman-god-goddess-beauty-legend-7494893/

***

John Lyly's *Sappho and Phao* Written c. 1582-84
    Earliest Extant Edition: 1584

***

This is a short, quick, and easy read.

Anecdotes are usually short humorous stories. Sometimes they are thought-provoking or informative, not amusing.

Educate Yourself
Read Like A Wolf Eats
Be Excellent to Each Other
Books Then, Books Now, Books Forever

***

In this retelling, as in all my retellings, I have tried to make the work of literature accessible to modern readers who may lack some of the knowledge about mythology, religion, and history that the literary work's contemporary audience had.

Do you know a language other than English? If you do, I give you permission to translate this book, copyright your translation, publish or self-publish it, and keep all the royalties for yourself. (Do give me credit, of course, for the original retelling.)

I would like to see my retellings of classic literature used in schools, so I give permission to the country of Finland (and all other countries) to get an eBook copy of this book and give copies to all students forever. I also give permission to the state of Texas (and all other states) to get an eBook copy of this book and give copies to all students forever. I also give permission to all teachers to get an eBook copy of this book and give copies to all students forever.

Teachers need not actually teach my retellings. Teachers are welcome to give students copies of my eBooks as background material. For example, if they are teaching Homer's *Iliad* and *Odyssey*, teachers are welcome to give students copies of my *Virgil's* Aeneid: *A Retelling in Prose* and tell students, "Here's another ancient epic you may want to read in your spare time."

CAST OF CHARACTERS

Phao, a young ferryman.

Sappho, princess of Syracuse.

LADIES OF SAPPHO'S COURT:

Mileta.

Lamia.

Ismena.

Canope.

Eugenua.

Favilla.

OTHER MORTAL CHARACTERS:

Trachinus, a courtier.

Criticus, page to Trachinus. A page is a boy-servant.

Pandion, a scholar.

Molus, page to Pandion.

Sybilla, an aged soothsayer.

GODS AND GODDESSES:

Venus, goddess of love and beauty and sexual passion.

Cupid, her son, god of love. He is young enough to be able to sit on a woman's lap.

Vulcan, her husband, the blacksmith god.

Calypho, one of the Cyclops.

SCENE: Syracuse, Sicily

NOTES:

In this society, a person of higher rank would use "thou," "thee," "thine," and "thy" when referring to a person of lower rank. (These terms were also used affectionately and between equals.) A person of lower rank would use "you" and "your" when referring to a person of higher rank.

The word "wench" at this time was not necessarily negative. It was often used affectionately.

The word "fair" can mean attractive, beautiful, handsome, good-looking.

ROMAN NAME (GREEK NAME)

Bacchus (Dionysus): god of wine and ecstasy

Ceres (Demeter): goddess of grain and agriculture

Cupid (Eros): god of love; also, son of Venus

Diana (Artemis): goddess of the hunt

Juno (Hera): wife of Jupiter, king of the gods, and so she is queen of the gods

Jupiter, aka Jove (Zeus): king of the gods

Mercury (Hermes): a messenger-god

Neptune (Poseidon): god of the sea

Proserpine (Persephone): wife of Pluto, god of the Land of the Dead; also, daughter of Ceres

Pluto (Hades): god of the Land of the Dead

Ulysses (Odysseus): hero of Homer's epic poem *Odyssey*

Venus (Aphrodite): goddess of sexual desire

Vesta (Hestia): goddess of the hearth

Vulcan (Hephaestus): the blacksmith god

EDITIONS

Peter Lukacs has excellently edited and annotated this play. It can be downloaded free here:

http://elizabethandrama.org/the-playwrights/john-lyly/sapho-and-phao-by-john-lyly/

***

David Bevington has also excellently edited and annotated this play:

Lyly, John. *Campaspe. Sappho and Phao.* The Revels Plays. *Campaspe* edited by G.K. Hunter. *Sappho and Phao* edited by David Bevington. Manchester, England and New York: Manchester University Press. 1991.

CHAPTER 1

— 1.1 —

Near his ferry that took passengers to Syracuse, Sicily, Phao said to himself:

"Thou are a ferryman, Phao, yet thou are a free man. Your riches are contentment, and your honors are a quiet mind. Thy thoughts are no higher than thy fortunes and luck, nor are thy desires greater than thy calling."

Phao was a ferryman, and he had no desire to be anything other than a ferryman.

Phao continued:

"He who climbs stands on glass and falls on thorn."

Glass is easily broken.

Phao continued:

"Thy heart's thirst is satisfied with thy hand's thrift, and thy gentle labors in the day turn to sweet slumbers in the night."

"Thy hand's thrift" means "thy hand's industry." Phao's income from his work was enough to supply him with what he wanted.

Phao continued:

"As much does it delight thee to rule thine oar in a calm stream as it does Sappho to sway the scepter in her splendid court and rule this city.

"Envy never casts her eye low, ambition points always upward, and revenge barks only at stars.

"Thou fare delicately, if thou have a fare to buy anything. Thine fishing pole is ready when thine oar is idle, and as sweet is the fish that thou catch in the river as the fowl that others buy in the market."

Phao had enough food. He ate well when he had a paying passenger, and if he didn't have a paying passenger, he ate the fish he caught from the river.

Phao continued:

"Thou need not fear poison in thy glass, nor treason in thy guard."

Many Roman emperors died of other than natural causes. The same is true of many medieval and Renaissance kings.

Phao continued:

"The wind is thy greatest enemy, whose might is withstood with policy: skillful navigation. Oh, sweet life, seldom found under a golden roof, but often found under a thatched cottage."

He saw someone coming and said:

"But here comes someone. I will go aside and listen; it may be a passenger."

Phao retired.

Venus and Cupid appeared on the scene. Venus is the goddess of sexual passion, and Cupid — her son — is the god of love. Cupid was carrying a bow and arrows.

They were traveling in the human realm and were not instantly recognizable as goddess and god.

Venus complained about her husband and her life. Her husband, Vulcan, was the blacksmith to the gods. His legs were crooked, but his arms and shoulders were strong.

Venus said:

"It is no less unseemly than unwholesome for Venus, who is most honored in princes' courts, to live with Vulcan in a blacksmith's forge, where bellows blow instead of lovers' sighs, dark smokes rise instead of sweet perfumes, and instead of the panting of loving hearts, is heard only the beating of steeled hammers.

"Unhappy is Venus. While carrying the fire of passion in thine own breast, thou must dwell with fire in his forge.

"What does Vulcan do all day but endeavor to be as crabbed in manners as he is crooked in body, driving nails when he should give kisses, and hammering hard armors when he should sing sweet amours — sweet love songs?

"It came by lot, not love, that I was linked with him."

According to Venus, the gods cast lots to determine whom she would marry.

A different account is that when Vulcan was born with crooked legs, his mother, Juno, queen of the gods, threw him down from Mount Olympus. He fell for a day, and then two sea nymphs, Thetis (mother of Achilles) and Eurynome, took care of him. Vulcan created a golden throne for Juno, and when she sat in it, shackles appeared and bound her to the throne. The only way that Jupiter, king of the gods and husband to Juno, could convince Vulcan to release Juno was to give him a wife: Venus.

Venus continued:

"He gives thee bolts, Cupid, instead of arrows, fearing perhaps (jealous fool that he is) that if he should give thee an arrowhead, he should make himself a broad head."

Bolts are short, blunt arrows.

Cupid shoots arrows into people's hearts. When one of his gold arrows hits a person's heart, that person falls in love.

Short, blunt arrows cannot pierce the heart.

A broad head is a head that has horns: the sign of a cuckold — a man with an unfaithful wife. Venus was joking that Vulcan was afraid to give Cupid real arrows because Cupid might shoot Venus in the heart with an arrow and make her fall in love with someone who would help her make Vulcan a cuckold.

Venus continued:

"But come, we will go to Syracuse, where thy deity shall be shown by your use of your arrows, and where my disdain for a woman who has never fallen in love shall be shown. I will yoke the neck that has yet never bowed, at which, if Jove repine and complain, Jove shall repent. Sappho shall know, no matter how beautiful Sappho is, that there is a Venus who can conquer, no matter how fortunate Sappho is."

Both Venus and Cupid wanted human beings to fall in love. That included beautiful, fortunate women such as Sappho, ruler of Syracuse, who had never fallen in love.

Cupid said, "If Jove spies Sappho, he will devise some new shape to entertain her."

Jove, aka Jupiter, like other gods, often had affairs with mortal women and with goddesses. The gods were shape-shifters, and because Jupiter had a jealous wife, he would sometimes change his shape in an attempt to hide an affair from her.

For example, Jove came to Leda while he was in the form of a swan. She gave birth to Helen of Troy.

For example, Jove came to Europa while he was in the form of a bull. She climbed on his back, and he carried her to the Island of Crete. She gave birth to King Minos of Crete. Europe was named after her.

For example, Jove came to Danae while he was in the form of a shower of gold. She gave birth to the hero Perseus.

"Strike thou Sappho, with an arrow," Venus said. "Let Jove devise what shape he can."

Cupid replied, "Mother, they say she keeps her thoughts on a lease to control them, that she conquers affections, and sends love up and down upon errands; I am afraid she will yerk — hit — me if I hit her with an arrow."

"Peevish boy, can mortal creatures resist that which the immortal gods cannot redress and remedy?" Venus asked.

The immortal gods cannot resist the effects of Cupid's arrows, and so mortal humans cannot resist the effects of his arrows.

"The gods are amorous, and therefore they are willing to be pierced," Cupid said.

Yes, pierced with an arrow, and in the case of the goddesses such as Venus, pierced sexually.

"And she is amiable, lovable, and worthy to be loved, and therefore she must be pierced," Venus said.

"I dare not shoot an arrow at her," Cupid said.

"Draw thine arrow to the head, else I will make thee repent it at the heart," Venus said. "Come along, and behold the ferry-boy who is ready to conduct us."

Phao stepped forward.

Venus asked, "Pretty youth, do you keep the ferry that bends its way to Syracuse?"

"This is the ferry, fair lady, that bends its way to Syracuse," Phao said.

"I fear, if the water should begin to swell and become rough, thou will lack the cunning needed to guide the ferry," Venus said.

After all, Phao was young.

"These waters are commonly as the passengers are," Phao said, "and therefore since I will be carrying one as fair in appearance as you, there is no cause to fear a rough sea."

"To pass the time in thy boat, can thou devise any pastime?" Venus asked.

"If the wind is with me, I can fish or tell tales; if the wind is against me, it will be a pleasure for you to see me take pains to steer the ferry," Phao said.

"I don't like fishing, yet I was born from the sea," Venus said.

A myth states that Venus was born in the sea foam by Paphos on the island of Cyprus.

"But he may bless fishing, whoever caught such a one as you in the sea," Phao said, complimenting Venus.

"It was not with a fishing pole, my boy, but with a net," Venus said.

"So, it was said that Vulcan caught Mars with Venus," Phao said.

Phao was referring to a comic story about Venus having an affair with Mars, god of war, and the two being caught in a net by Vulcan, Venus' husband.

"Did thou hear about that?" Venus said. "It was some tale."

It was quite a tale, but Venus was not eager to speak about it.

"Yes, madam," Phao said, "and in the boat I did mean to make that my tale."

Did Phao know who Venus was? He was standing near Venus and Cupid as they talked, and their conversation revealed their identities. If Phao knew who Venus was, he was naïve to think that she wanted to hear that tale.

Venus said:

"It is not for a ferryman to talk about the gods' loves, but to tell how thy father could dig and thy mother spin.

"But come, let us go now."

"I am ready to wait on — to serve — you," Phao said.

They exited.

— 1.2 —

Trachinus (a courtier), Criticus (Trachinus' page), Pandion (a scholar), and Molus (Pandion's servant) entered the scene that Phao, Venus, and Cupid had just vacated.

Trachinus said, "Pandion, since your coming from the university to the court, from the universities of Athens to Syracuse, how do you feel yourself altered, either in humor or opinion?"

"Humor" can mean mood, disposition, or temperament.

Pandion replied, "I am altered, Trachinus. I have changed. I say no more, and I am ashamed that anyone should know so much."

Trachinus said:

"Here you see as great virtue and far greater splendor: Here is the action of that which you contemplate. I mean Sappho. She is beautiful by nature, royal by birth, learned by education, politic and prudent by self-government, and rich by peace."

Peace does have its financial advantages. Witness the waste in the Russia-Ukraine war.

Trachinus continued:

"It is hard to judge whether she is more beautiful or wise, more virtuous or fortunate.

"Besides, in this place, don't you look on fair ladies instead of good letters, and behold fair faces instead of fine phrases?"

"Good letters" is good literature and good scholarship.

Trachinus continued:

"In universities, virtues and vices are only shadowed in colors, white and black.

"But in courts, virtues and vices are shown to the life, good and bad."

In university, virtues and vices are studied using theories.

But in courts, virtues and vices are acted out in real life.

Trachinus continued:

"There in Athenian universities, times past are read of in old books, times present are set down by new devices and with new ideas, and times to come are conjectured at by aim, by prophecy, or by chance.

"But here in the royal court, are times in perfection, not by device, as fables, but in execution, as truths."

In Athenian universities, times past can be read about in old books, times present are written about in new books, and times future are guessed about.

But in the royal court, the times are being created. In the royal court, actions are being performed that the universities will write about.

Trachinus continued:

"Believe me, Pandion, in Athens you have only tombs; in court we have the bodies.

"You have the pictures of Venus and the wise goddesses; we have the persons and the virtues.

"What has a scholar found out by study that a courtier has not found out by practice? Foolish are you who think to see more at the candle-snuff than the sunbeams, to sail further in a little brook than in the main ocean, to make a greater harvest by gleaning — gathering — ears of corn left behind by reapers than reaping full fields.

"What do you say, Pandion, isn't all this true?"

Two kinds of life exist: a life of action and a life of contemplation. Trachinus led the life of action in the court of Syracuse, and he extolled that life to Pandion, who had been living a life of contemplation in the Athenian universities.

"Trachinus, what more would you want?" Pandion said. "All that you say is true."

"Cease then to lead thy life in a study, constructed by pinning together a few boards to form partitions, and endeavor to be a courtier and live under embossed, delicately carved roofs," Trachinus said.

Pandion replied, "That would be a labor intolerable for Pandion."

"Why?" Trachinus asked.

"Because it is harder to shape a life to dissemble, than to go forward with the liberty of truth," Pandion answered.

Many royal courts contain factions that compete against each other for royal favors.

"Why, do you think that in court dissembling has any use?" Trachinus asked.

"Do you know in court any who intend to live?" Pandion asked.

Of course, all of us want to live, as long as we can be happy.

A proverb stated, "He that cannot dissemble knows not how to live (or rule)."

"You have no reason for saying so, except an old report," Trachinus said.

"Report does not have always a blister on her tongue," Pandion said.

A proverb stated, "Report has a blister on her tongue."

"Report" means idle talk and gossip.

Sometimes, proverbs state the truth. The same is true of reports and gossip.

"Aye, but this is the court of Sappho, nature's miracle, a court that resembles the tree salurus, whose root is fastened upon knotted steel, and in whose top bud leaves of pure gold," Trachinus said.

The tree salurus does not exist, but it is a symbol of a firm, stable foundation that gives rise to metaphorical golden fruit.

"Yet has salurus blasts and water boughs, worms and caterpillars," Pandion said.

"Blasts" are "blights."

"Water boughs" are water-shoots growing from the tree's roots that starve the tree of sap.

"Worms and caterpillars" are parasites.

"The virtue of the tree is not the reason for the tree's defects, but the easterly wind, which is thought commonly to bring cankers and rottenness," Trachinus said.

In Genesis 41:6, the Pharoah dreamed of *"seven thin ears [of corn] blasted with the east wind"* (Bishop's Bible).

"Cankers" are destructive caterpillars.

"Nor is the excellency of Sappho the reason for rottenness at court, but the iniquity and evil of flatterers, who always whisper in princes' ears suspicion and sourness," Pandion said.

"Why, then you conclude with me that Sappho for virtue has no copartner — no equal," Trachinus said.

"Yes, and with the judgment of the world, that she is without comparison," Pandion said.

Pandion greatly criticized life at the court, but he greatly respected Sappho.

"We will take the ferry and go there to the court immediately," Trachinus said.

"I wish I might return to the Athenian universities immediately," Pandion said.

He wanted to return to a life of scholarly contemplation.

"Why, there you may live still," Trachinus said.

By "still," he meant "always."

"But not still," Pandion said.

By "still," he meant "at peace."

"How do you like the ladies?" Trachinus asked. "Aren't they surpassingly beautiful?"

"My eye drinks neither the color of wine nor women," Pandion said.

Women's "color" is often makeup.

"Yet I am sure that in judgment you are not so severe, but that you can be content to praise beauty by day or by night," Trachinus said.

Pandion said:

"When I behold beauty before the sun, the sun's beams dim beauty.

"When I behold beauty by candle, beauty obscures candlelight.

"The result is that at no time can I judge because at any time I cannot discern because in the sun is a brightness that casts a shadow over beauty, and because in beauty is a glistening brilliance that extinguishes light by outshining it."

"You spoke like a scholar," Trachinus said. "You flatter that which you seem to mislike, and you seem to disgrace that which you most marvel at. But let us leave now."

"Mislike" means dislike without a good reason.

Pandion said:

"I will follow you."

He then said to Molus, his servant:

"And you, sir boy, go to Syracuse round about by land, where you shall meet my baggage, pay for the carriage, and convey my baggage to my lodging."

Molus would not take the ferry; he would instead walk around the harbor.

"I think all your stuff consists of bundles of paper," Trachinus said, "but now you must learn to turn your library into a wardrobe and see whether your rapier will hang better by your side, than the pen did in your car."

Pandion would need new clothes and a rapier to wear at court. Trachinus thought that Pandion should sell his books to get money to buy a new wardrobe.

Trachinus and Pandion exited.

The servants Criticus and Molus remained behind.

— 1.3 —

Criticus and Molus discussed their lives. Criticus was the page of Trachinus the courier, and Molus was the page of Pandion the scholar.

Criticus said, "Molus, what is the difference between thy common diet in Athens, and thy diet in court? What is the difference between a page's life, and a scholar's life?"

Molus replied, "This is the difference: There at the Athenian universities, of a little I had something; here in Syracuse, of a great deal I have nothing. There I wore pantofles —slippers — on my legs; here I bear them in my hands."

He carried his master's slippers to his master when they were needed.

Criticus said:

"Thou may be skilled in thy logic, but not in thy liripoop — thy commonsense knowledge. Most likely, no meat can go down your gullet, unless you have a knife to cut it."

He was saying that Molus could not digest new knowledge and a new lifestyle without first having thoroughly (and unnecessarily) examined it.

Criticus continued:

"But come among us, and you shall see us once in a morning have a mouse at a bay."

An animal that is at bay is forced to turn and face its enemies.

"A mouse?" Molus said. "Unproperly spoken."

A "mouse" can be a woman.

"Aptly understood, a mouse of beef," Criticus said.

The word "mouse" can also mean "muscle." "A mouse of beef" is a piece of beef.

Molus said:

"I think indeed a piece of beef as big as a mouse serves a great company of such cats."

"Such cats" may be metaphorical polecats: couriers.

Molus continued:

"But what else?"

Criticus said, "For other sports: A square die in a page's pocket is as decent and as fitting as a square cap on a graduate's head."

13

A square die is a cubed die used in gambling.

Molus said:

"You courtiers are mad fellows!

"We silly — that is, we simple — souls are only plodders at logic and arguments that conclude with 'therefore' — that is, *ergo.* Our wits are clasped up with our books; and so full of learning are we at home that we scarcely know good manners when we come abroad. We are cunning in nothing but in making small things great by figures, pulling on with the sweat of our studies a great shoe upon a little foot, burning out one candle in seeking for another.

"We are raw wordlings in matters of substance, but we are surpassingly good wranglers about shadows."

In other words: Scholars know little about the real world, but they can talk very well about things that are of little concern in the real world.

Criticus said:

"Then to be a scholar is time lost. We pages are politicians: For whatever we hear our masters talk of, we decide and settle; where we suspect, we undermine and ruin; and where we mislike for some particular grudge, there we pick quarrels for a general grievance."

A proverb stated, "One particularity concludes no generality."

Couriers' pages joined in the factionalism at court.

Criticus continued:

"No greetings are among us except instead of saying, 'Good morning,' we ask, 'What is the news?'

"We fall from cogging (cheating at dice) to cogging (flattering) statesmen; and so forward are men of middle rank in those matters that they would be cocks to tread down and crush and ruin others before they would be chickens to raise themselves.

"Youths are very forward to stroke their chins, although they have no beards, and to lie as loud as the man who has lived longest."

"These are the golden days!" Molus said.

"Then they are very dark days, for I can see no gold," Criticus said.

"You are gross-witted, master courtier," Molus said.

"And you, master scholar, are slender-witted," Criticus said.

"Gross-witted" and "slender-witted" both mean "stupid."

The university page and the court page are similar in some ways.

Molus said, "I meant that these are the times that were prophesied to be golden for an abundance of all things: sharpness of wit, excellency in knowledge, policy in government, for —"

"Whoa, *scholaris*," Criticus said. "I deny your argument."

"*Scholaris*" means 1) belonging to a school, and 2) scholar.

"Why, I was not making an argument," Molus said.

Criticus said:

"Then I deny it because it is no argument.

"But let us go and follow our masters."

Mileta, Lamia, Favilla, Ismena, Canope, and Eugenua — all of whom were ladies of Sappho's court — talked together. They were discussing how Venus had made Phao very handsome, and how Phao had fallen victim to improper pride.

"Isn't it strange that Phao suddenly should be so handsome?" Mileta said.

By "strange," she meant "odd."

"It cannot be strange, since Venus was disposed to make him fair," Lamia said. "That cunning would have been better bestowed on women, which would have deserved the thanks of nature."

By "strange," Lamia meant "unaccountable."

She wished that Venus had made women beautiful rather than make Phao handsome. It is women's nature to want to be beautiful.

"Perhaps she did it to spite women, or to scorn nature," Ismena said.

Canope said, referring to Phao:

"Proud elf!"

Phao was perhaps small; in any case, 'elf' was meant derogatively.

Canope continued:

"How squeamish — reserved and distant — he has become already, using both disdainful looks and imperious words, to such an extent that he galls with ingratitude. And then, ladies, you know how it cuts and distresses a woman to become a wooer."

Phao had become so good-looking that ladies wooed him. They chased him instead of being chased by him.

"Tush!" Eugenua said. "Children and fools, the fairer they are, the sooner they yield; an apple will catch the one, and a baby doll will catch the other."

"Your lover, I think, is a fair fool, for you love nothing but fruit and puppets," Ismena said.

"Puppets" are dolls.

In other words: Anyone who loves Eugenua would be a fool, for she loves apples and baby dolls. So said Ismena.

"I laugh at that which you all call 'love,' and I judge it to be only a word called 'love.' I think liking, a curtsy, a smile, a beck, and such-like are the very quintessence of love," Mileta said.

A "beck" is a beckoning, as with a finger.

Favilla said, "Aye, Mileta, but if you were as wise as you would like to be thought fair, or as fair as you think yourself wise, you would be as ready to please men, as you are reluctant to preen and dress up yourself; and as anxious to be thought amorous, as you are willing to be thought discreet."

In other words: A wise woman will try to please men. So said Favilla.

Mileta responded:

"No, no; men are good souls (the poor souls) who never inquire but with their eyes, loving to father the cradle, although they only mother the child."

In other words: Men love to father children (by having sex), but they leave the raising of the child to the mother.

Mileta continued:

"Give me their gifts, not their virtues: a grain of their gold weighs down a pound of their wit; a dram of 'give me' is heavier than an ounce of 'hear me.' Believe me, ladies, 'give' is a pretty thing."

Mileta liked to receive gifts from men; receiving gifts is so much better than hearing men talk.

Ismena said:

"I cannot help but often smile to myself to hear men call us weak vessels, when they prove themselves to be broken-hearted, and I cannot help but often smile to myself to hear them call us frail and weak-minded when their thoughts cannot hang together because men are scatter-minded.

"Men take pains to use words to flatter, and to use bribes — gifts — to allure; when we commonly and customarily wish their tongues were in their purses because they speak so simple-mindedly; and we wish that their proposals were in their bellies because they make them so peevishly."

Ismena would like men to eat their words and not talk rather than say their words.

Mileta said:

"It is good entertainment to see them lack the correct courting manner and have nothing to say to the purpose: for then they fall to good manners, having nothing in their mouths but 'sweet mistress,' wearing our hands out with courtly kissings, when their wits fail in courtly discourses."

When men don't have good courting conversation, they engage in compliments and hand-kisses.

Mileta continued: "Now ruffling their hairs, now setting their ruffs — pleated collars — in good order, then gazing with their eyes, and then sighing with a secret wring by the hand, all while thinking us likely to be wowed — won — by signs and ceremonies."

"Secret wrings by the hand" are "secret squeezings of the lady's hand."

Eugenua said, "Yet we, when we swear with our mouths we are not in love, then we sigh from the heart and pine in love."

Canope said:

"We are mad wenches if men pay attention to our words.

"For when I say, 'I wish no one cared for love more than I,' what I mean is 'I wish no one loved but I.'"

In other words: She says that she wishes all women were like herself indifferent to love, but she means that she wishes that she were the only woman to love and be loved.

Canope continued:

"Where we cry, 'Away!' don't we say, 'Go to'? And when men strive for kisses, we exclaim, 'Let us alone,' in a tone that suggests we would fall to that ourselves."

"Go to" can mean 1) Bah, or 2) Get down to it.

"Let us alone" can mean 1) Don't bother us, or 2) Leave it to us.

In other words: Women say one thing and mean the opposite.

Favilla said, "Nay, then, Canope, it is time to go — and behold Phao."

"Behold" can mean 1) see, and 2) consider.

"And" can be a conjunction that means "in order to."

"Where?" Ismena said, understanding "behold" to mean "see."

Favilla answered, "In your head, Ismena, nowhere else. But let us keep on our way and go to court."

"Wisely," Ismena said.

CHAPTER 2

— 2.1 —

At nighttime, in front of Sybilla's cave, Phao arrived, carrying a small mirror: the sign of a vain man. Sybilla, a prophetess, was sitting in her cave.

Previously, Phao had been a contented man, but now he was unhappy.

He said to himself, "Phao, thy mean fortune and lack of wealth causes thee to use an oar and make a living, and thy sudden beauty causes thee to use a mirror: By the one is seen thy need, and in the other is seen thy pride.

"Oh, Venus! In thinking thou have blessed me, thou have cursed me, adding to a poor estate a proud heart; and to a disdained man a disdaining mind."

"Thou do not flatter thyself, Phao, that thou are fair. Fair? I fear that 'fair' is a word too foul for a face so surpassingly fair."

Venus had made Phao extraordinarily good-looking, and Phao recognized that he had grown proud. People looked down on him because of his lack of wealth, but Phao looked down on them because of their lack of beauty. He knew that this was wrong, but he could not control his pride.

Phao continued:

"But what avails beauty? What good is it?

"If thou had all the things thou would wish for, thou might die tomorrow; and if thou lacked all things thou desire, thou shall live until thou die.

"Tush, Phao! There has grown more pride in thy mind than attractiveness in thy face.

"Blush from shame, foolish boy, to think thine own thoughts: Cease complaining, and crave counsel. Find someone to give you good advice.

"And look! Behold Sybilla sitting in the mouth of her cave.

"I will greet her."

He said to Sybilla:

"Lady, I am afraid that I am out of my way and headed the wrong direction in life, and I am so benighted in my thoughts that I am compelled to ask you for your advice."

The time was also literally night.

Sybilla replied, "Fair youth, if you will be advised by me, you shall at this time seek no other inn than my cave because it is no less perilous to travel by night than it is uncomfortable and disquieting."

"Your courtesy that you have offered me has anticipated what my necessity was going to make me entreat from you," Phao said.

Sybilla said:

"Come near, take a stool, and sit down."

Phao did that.

Sybilla continued:

"Now, because these winter nights are long, and because children delight in nothing more than to hear old wives' tales, we will beguile and pass the time with some story.

"And although you see wrinkles and furrows in my tawny face, yet you may perhaps find wisdom and counsel in my white hairs."

Her face was tawny: blotched from old-age spots.

"Lady, nothing can content me better than a tale," Phao said. "Neither is there anything more necessary for me than counsel and advice."

"Were you born so good-looking by nature?" Sybilla asked.

"No, I was made so good-looking by Venus," Phao said.

"For what reason?" Sybilla asked.

"I fear it was meant to be some curse," Phao said.

"Why? Do you love and cannot obtain your love?" Sybilla asked.

"No, I may obtain love, but I cannot love," Phao said.

Women loved him, but he did not return their love.

"Be careful about that, my child!" Sybilla said.

Not returning love can be a bad thing, as can being unable to love.

"I cannot choose otherwise, good madam," Phao said.

"Then listen to my tale, which I hope shall be as a straight thread to lead you out of those crooked conceits, and place you in the plain, clear path of love," Sybilla said.

The half-bull, half-man monster known as the Minotaur was kept in a labyrinth on Crete, Theseus, a hero from Athens, undertook to kill the Minotaur, and he found help from the Cretan princess Ariadne, who gave him a spool of thread which he unwound as he moved in the labyrinth. After he had killed the Minotaur, he followed the thread back to the entrance of the labyrinth.

"I am listening," Phao said.

Sybilla said:

"When I was young, as you now are, I say without boasting that I was as beautiful as you, for Phoebus Apollo in his godhead sought to get my maidenhead."

Apollo is the god who drives the Sun-chariot across the sky each day. The immortal gods often had affairs with mortal women, and Apollo wanted to take Sybilla's virginity when she was a young woman.

Sybilla continued:

"But I, who was a foolish wench, receiving a benefit from above, began to grow squeamish beneath."

The benefit from a heavenly god was his notice, but then she grew squeamish here below on the earth and below her waist. She would also ask for a gift from the god.

Sybilla continued:

"This was not unlike the plant named asolis, which being made green by heavenly drops, shrinks into the ground when there fall showers, and it was not unlike the Syrian mud, which being made white chalk by the sun, never ceases rolling until it lies in the shadow.

"To sweet prayers, Apollo added great promises. I, either desirous to make trial of his power, or willing to prolong my own life, caught up a handful of sand, consenting to his suit if I might live as many years as there were grains of sand.

"Phoebus Apollo (for what cannot gods do, and what for love will they not do?) granted my petition.

"And then — I sigh and blush to tell the rest — I revoked and did not keep my promise to sleep with him."

"Wasn't the god angry to see you unkind and ungenerous?" Phao asked.

"He was angry, my boy, which was the reason that I became unfortunate," Sybilla said.

"What revenge for such rigor — such hard-heartedness — do the gods give?" Phao asked.

"None but allowing us to live and know we are no gods," Sybilla said.

The gods are eternally the same age. Jupiter will always be a mature man. Apollo will always be a young man. Cupid will always be a youth.

Sybilla, who was not a goddess, was now a very old and much wrinkled woman.

"Please continue," Phao said.

Sybilla said:

"I will.

"Having received long life by Phoebus Apollo and splendid beauty by nature, I thought all the year would have been May, that fresh colors would always continue, that time and fortune could not wear out what gods and nature had wrought up.

"Not once did I imagine that white and red should return to black and yellow.

The colors were the color of her complexion when young and then when old. This kind of returning foreshadows returning to dust after life ends.

Sybilla continued:

"Not once did I imagine that the juniper, the longer it grew, the crookeder it would grow.

"And not once did I imagine that in a face without blemish, there would come a countless number of wrinkles.

"I did in the past as you do now. I went about with my mirror, ravished with the pride of my own beauty; and you shall do in the future as I do now. You shall be loath to see a mirror, disdaining the deformity of old age.

"There were none who heard about my fault, but shunned my favor, to such an extent that I stooped because of age before I tasted of youth. I was sure to be long-lived, but not certain to be beloved."

Sybilla's fault was not keeping her promise to Apollo. Knowing the power of the gods, people shunned her and did not become romantically involved with her.

Sybilla continued:

"Gentlemen who used to sigh from their hearts for my sweet love, began to point with their fingers at my withered face, and they laughed to see the eyes, out of which fire seemed to sparkle, to be assisted, being old, with spectacles.

"This caused me to withdraw myself to a solitary cave, where I must lead six hundred years in no less mourning of crabbed age than grief of remembered youth."

Because of her fault, Sybilla had been unable to enjoy her youth.

Sybilla continued:

"I have only this comfort, that having ceased to be fair, I study to be wise, wishing to be thought a grave matron, since I cannot return to be a young maiden."

Sybilla had asked for a very long life, but she had not asked to be youthful for all those years, so she grows older and older and older, with all the disadvantages of old age.

"Isn't it possible to die before you become so old?" Phao asked.

"No more possible than it is for me to return as you are, to be as young as you," Sybilla said.

"Couldn't you settle your fancy upon any, or would your destiny not allow it?" Phao asked.

In other words: Were you able to find anyone to love?

"Women willingly ascribe that to fortune, which wittingly was committed by frowardness and perversity," Sybilla replied.

In other words: She had not.

"What will you have me do?" Phao asked.

Sybilla answered:

"Take heed you don't do as I did.

"Don't make too much of fading beauty, which is fair in the cradle and foul in the grave; resembling polyon, whose leaves are white in the morning and blue before night; or anyta, which is a sweet flower at the rising of the sun but becomes a weed if it is not plucked before the setting of the sun.

"Fair faces have no fruits if they have no witnesses.

"When you shall behold over this tender flesh a tough skin, when your eyes, which were accustomed to glance at others' faces, will be sunk so hollow that you can scarcely look out of your own head, and when all your teeth shall wag — wiggle — as fast as your tongue, then you will repent the time that you cannot call back and be forced to bear what most you blame and find fault with."

"What most you blame and find fault with" is the knowledge of wasted opportunities in the past.

"Don't lose the pleasant time of your youth, than which there is nothing swifter, nothing sweeter.

"Beauty is a slippery good, which decreases while it is increasing, resembling the medlar, which in the moment of its full ripeness, is known to be in a rottenness."

Medlars are apples that were eaten when they were soft and pulpy: As soon as they were ripe, they were rotten.

Beauty decreased while it is increasing.

In other words: You may grow more beautiful in the course of a year, but that is one year fewer of the years you will be beautiful.

Sybilla continued:

"While you look in the mirror, your beauty grows old with time; if you look at the sun, your beauty becomes parched with heat; if your beauty faces the wind, it is blasted with cold.

"Beauty takes a great deal of care to keep it, you have a short space to enjoy it, and suddenly you lose it.

"Don't be coy and shy when you are courted.

"Fortune's wings are made of time's feathers, which don't stay while one may measure them.

"Be affable and courteous in youth, so that you may be honored in age.

"Roses that lose their colors still keep their smells, and plucked from the stalk, they are distilled into sweet-smelling rose oil.

"The plant cotonea, because it bows when the sun rises, is sweetest when it is oldest; and children who in their tender years sow courtesy shall in their declining states reap compassion.

"Don't be proud of beauty's painting whose colors consume themselves, because they are beauty's painting."

Beauty's painting is youth's natural coloring. It doesn't last, just like another kind of painting — cosmetic makeup — doesn't last.

Phao said, "I am driven by your counsel into diverse thoughts, neither knowing how to stand, nor where to fall; but to yield to love is the only thing I hate."

Sybilla's advice was to seek a mean between extremes. Enjoy your beauty, but don't overvalue it. In your youth, know that you will someday become old, so act in such a way in your youth that people will feel compassion for you when you are old.

Sybilla had also said not to be coy and shy when someone courted you.

Sybilla said:

"I commit you to Lady Fortune, who is likely to play such pranks with you as your tender years can scarcely bear, nor your green, naïve wits understand."

As a prophetess, Sibylla could foresee the future. Also, as a prophetess, Sibylla spoke vaguely about the future and gave vague advice. In this case, Sibylla knew that Phao, who was lowly born, and Sappho, who was highly born, would fall in love. Phao would become a member of the court, and he would be exposed to the envy of other, more worldly members of the court. Not all loves result in happiness.

She added:

"But return to me often, and if I cannot remove the bad effects of what may happen to you, yet I will manifest and reveal the reasons why they happen to you."

"I go, and I am ready to return for advice before I make a decision about what I will do," Phao said.

Sybilla said:

"Yet listen to two words."

Like many prophetesses, Sybilla had many more than two words left to say.

She continued:

"Thou shall get friendship by dissembling, and thou shall get love by hatred.

"Unless thou perish, thou shall perish.

"In digging for a stone, thou shall reach a star.

"Thou shall be hated most because thou are loved most.

"Thy death shall be feared and wished."

Sybilla seemed to be saying this: To survive and flourish as a member of the court, Phao would have to learn to dissemble. This would involve a change: a perishing of his old self so that he will not become a victim of other dissemblers at court. Phao would rise high, but at the cost of being a member of a court beset by factions, many of whose members will maliciously envy him.

Sybilla continued:

"So much for prophecy, which nothing can prevent.

"Now hear this for counsel, which thou may follow.

"Don't keep company with ants that have wings."

Winged ants are aspirers. Ants are an earthly species, but winged ants attempt to rise above their assigned place in the natural order.

Sybilla continued:

"Nor talk with anyone near the hill of a mole."

In this society, moles were thought to possess a keen sense of hearing. Phao needed to stay away from those who would spy on him. Such spies were often informers who would twist and deliberately misinterpret what they had heard.

Sybilla continued:

"Where thou smell the sweetness of serpent's breath, beware. Don't touch any part of the body."

In other words: Don't be seduced by flatterers.

Sybilla continued:

"Don't be merry among those who put bugloss in their wine, and sugar in thine."

Bugloss is a medicinal herb, and sugar is used to make bad wine taste better.

Sybilla continued:

"If anyone talks about the eclipse of the sun, say thou never saw it."

Eclipses are bad omens, often foretelling the deaths of princes.

Sybilla continued:

"Nourish no conies in thy vaults, nor swallows in thine eaves."

Conies are rabbits; they are also con men and flatterers. Vaults are storage rooms for wine. Swallows fly away in the winter, just as false friends fly away when someone — such as Phao — is having hard times.

Sybilla continued:

"Sow next to thy vines mandrake plants."

Mandrake was thought to prevent grape vines from making too-sharp wine.

Sybilla continued:

"And always keep thine ears open, and thy mouth shut.

"Always keep thine eyes upward toward heaven, and thy fingers down."

Sibylla was warning Phao from becoming too greedy.

Sybilla continued:

"So shall thou do better than otherwise, although never as well as I wish for thee."

Phao had a friend in his corner.

Phao said:

"Alas! Madam, your prophecy threatens miseries, and your counsel urges impossibilities."

The prophecy was mostly bad, and the advice difficult or impossible to take.

Sybilla said, "Farewell, I can answer no more."

She exited into her cave.

Phao remained.

Sappho, Trachinus the courier, Pandion the scholar, Criticus (Trachinus' page), and Molus (Pandion's page) walked over to Phao.

Phao said to himself:

"Unhappy Phao!

"But hold on, what gallant troupe of people is this?

"What gentlewoman is this?"

Overhearing Phao, Criticus said, "She is Sappho, a lady here in Sicily."

"What good-looking boy is that?" Sappho asked.

"Phao, the ferryman of Syracuse," Trachinus said.

"I never saw anyone more splendid," Phao said. "Are all ladies of such majesty?"

"No, this is she whom all wonder at and worship," Criticus said.

"I have seldom seen a sweeter face," Sappho said. "Are all ferrymen of that fairness?"

"No, madam, this is the man whom Venus determined among men to make the best looking," Trachinus said.

"Seeing that I have come forth only to take the air, I will cross on the ferry and go to the fields and then go in through the park," Sappho said. "I think the walk will be pleasant."

The park was an enclosed hunting reserve for the royal family.

"You will much delight in the flattering green, which now begins to be in its glory," Trachinus said.

The pleasing vegetation was beginning to bloom.

"Sir boy, will you undertake to carry us over the water?" Sappho asked.

Phao stared at her, mesmerized by her beauty.

Sappho asked, "Are you dumb? Can't you speak?"

"Madam, I beg your pardon," Phao said. "I am spurblind: I could scarcely see."

"Spurblind" was Phao's variant of "purblind." Phao was partially blind because of Sappho's beauty, which was spurring him into falling in love with her.

"It is a pity that in so good a face there should be an evil eye," Sappho said.

She was bewitched by Phao.

"I wish in my face there were never an eye," Phao said.

He had seen Sappho's beauty and fallen in love, something that he had said he did not want to do.

Both Sappho and Phao had fallen in love at first sight.

"Thou can never be rich in a trade of life of all the basest," Sappho said.

Ferrymen tend not to become rich.

"Yet I am content, madam, which is a kind of life of all the best," Phao said.

"Will thou forsake the ferry, and follow the court as a page?" Sappho asked.

"As it pleases Lady Fortune, madam, to whom I am an apprentice," Phao said.

"Come, let's go," Sappho said.

"Will you go, Pandion?" Trachinus said.

"Yes," Pandion said.

All exited except Molus and Criticus, who remained behind. Criticus walked over to Molus.

<h1 style="text-align:center">— 2.3 —</h1>

Molus said:

"Criticus comes in good time. I shall not be alone.

"What is the news, Criticus?"

"I taught you that lesson, to ask what is the news, and this is the news," Criticus said. "Tomorrow there shall be a desperate fray between two men, made at all weapons — that is, no holds barred — from the brown bill to the bodkin."

A brown bill is a long brown handle with an axe-head and a spear point at one end.

A bodkin is a dagger.

Molus said, "Now that thou talk about frays, please tell me, what is that which they talk about so commonly in court — valor, the stab, the pistol — for the which every man who dares is so much honored?"

Criticus said:

"Oh, Molus, beware of valor!

"He who can look big and threatening; who wears his dagger pommel lower than the point; who maintains a good defensive position and can hit a small target such as a button with a thrust of a sword or dagger; and who will willingly go into the dueling field man to man for a bout or two — he, Molus, is a shrewd fellow and shall be well-followed with admirers."

In real life, anyone who puts his dagger in a sheath with the point pointing up and the hilt pointing down will find it difficult to take out the dagger.

"What is the end of it all?" Molus asked.

"Danger or death," Criticus said.

"If it is only death that brings all this commendation, I regard the person who is killed with a surfeit to be as valiant as the person who is killed with a sword," Molus said.

A surfeit is overeating and/or overdrinking.

"How so?" Criticus asked.

Molus replied:

"If I venture upon a full stomach to eat a rasher on the coals, eat a carbonado, drink a carouse, swallow all things that may procure sickness or death, am I not as valiant to die so in a house, as the other is valiant to die in a dueling field?"

A rasher on the coals is a slice of broiled bacon or ham.

A carbonado is a piece of cross-cut and grilled meat.

A carouse is a full cup of a drink containing alcohol.

Molus continued:

"I think that epicures are as desperate and reckless as soldiers, and cooks provide as good weapons as cutlers."

Cutlers make knives.

Epicures seek pleasure in life. The philosopher Epicurus, however, believed in moderation because excesses lead to less pleasure.

"Oh, valiant knight!" Criticus said.

"I will die for this opinion," Molus said. "What greater valor is there?"

"This is how scholars fight, who seek to choke their stomachs rather than see their blood," Criticus said.

"Choke their stomach" can mean 1) cram their stomachs with food, or 2) stop their stomachs — their appetites — for dueling.

"I will stand upon this point: If it is valor to dare to die, then a man is valiant howsoever he dies," Molus said.

"Well, let's talk more about this hereafter, but here comes Calypho — we will have some entertainment."

Calypho entered the scene.

Calypho was a Cyclops who helped Vulcan make thunderbolts for Jupiter, king of the gods.

He was looking for Venus, who gads about here and there. She was unpopular among Vulcan's Cyclopes.

He said:

"My mistress, I think, has got a gadfly. She is never at home, and yet none can tell where she is outside her home. My master Vulcan was a 'wise' man when he matched with and married such a woman. When she comes into Vulcan's forge, we must put out the fire because of the smoke, we must hang up our hammers because of the noise, and we must do no work except wait on her and get her what she wants.

"She is beautiful, but by my truth I swear I doubt her honesty and chastity.

"I must seek her, her whom I fear Mars has found."

Loyalty means faithfulness.

Chastity does not mean "no sex"; it means "only ethical sex, if any."

A husband and wife are chaste if they sleep only with each other; however, Calypho feared that Venus slept with other gods and mortals in addition to sleeping with her husband.

"Whom do thou seek?" Criticus asked.

"I have found those I don't seek," Calypho said.

Those he had found, of course, were Criticus and Molus.

"I hope you have found those who are honest and truth-telling," Molus said.

"It may be, but I seek no such," Calypho said.

He was seeking Venus, not someone who was honest and truth-telling.

"Criticus, you shall see me by the use of my learning prove Calypho to be the devil," Molus said.

"Let us see," Criticus said, "but I ask thee to please prove it better than thou did prove thyself to be valiant."

"Calypho, I will prove thee to be the devil," Molus said.

"Then will I swear thee to be a god," Calypho said.

"The devil is black," Molus said.

"What do I care?" Calypho said.

"Thou are black," Molus said.

"What do you care?" Calypho said.

"Therefore, thou are the devil," Molus said.

"I deny that," Calypho said.

"It is the conclusion of my argument," Molus said. "Thou must not deny it."

Of course, Molus had made a bad argument because not all black things are the devil:

Premise 1: The devil is black.

Premise 2: Calypho is black.

Conclusion: Calypho is the devil.

"In spite of all conclusions, I will deny it," Calypho said.

"Molus, the blacksmith holds you hard," Criticus said. "He denies your argument."

"Thou see he has no reason," Molus said. "He knows no logic."

"Try him again," Criticus said.

"I will reason with thee now from a place," Molus said.

"From a place" meant "from a proverb or other well-known saying."

"I mean to answer you in no other place than here," Calypho said.

"Like master, like serving-man," Molus said.

"It may be," Calypho said.

"But thy master has horns," Molus said.

"And so may thou," Calypho said.

Calypho meant that Molus could one day have the horns of a cuckold: a man with an unfaithful wife.

"Therefore, thou have horns, and *ergo*, thou are a devil," Molus said.

This is another bad argument:

Premise 1: Vulcan has horns.

Premise 2: Like master, like serving-man.

Premise 3: Calypso is a serving-man to Vulcan.

Conclusion: Calypho has horns.

Premise 1: Calypho has horns.

Premise 2: Devils have horns.

Conclusion: Calypho is a devil.

"Are all who have horns devils?" Calypho asked.

"All men who have horns are," Molus said.

"Then there are more devils on earth than in hell," Calypho said.

Hmm. There must a lot of cuckolds on earth.

"But what do thou answer?" Molus asked.

"I deny that," Calypho said.

"Thou deny what?" Molus asked.

Calypho said:

"Whatsoever it is that shall prove me a devil.

"But listen, scholar, I am a plain fellow, and I can make nothing but with the hammer.

"What will thou say, if I prove that thee are a blacksmith?"

"Then I will say thou are a scholar," Molus said.

"Prove it, Calypho, and I will give thee a good *colaphum*," Criticus said.

A *colaphum* is a blow.

"I will prove it or else —" Calypho said.

"Or else what?" Criticus asked.

Calypho said:

"Or else I will not prove it.

"Thou are a blacksmith; therefore, thou are a blacksmith.

"The conclusion, you say, must not be denied, and therefore, it is true: Thou are a blacksmith."

This is the argument:

Premise 1: Molus is a blacksmith.

Conclusion: Molus is a blacksmith.

If the premise is true, then the conclusion is true, and if the conclusion is true, the premise is true.

"Aye, but I deny your antecedent," Molus said.

The argument can be framed as a conditional statement with an antecedent and a consequent:

If Molus is a blacksmith, then Molus is a blacksmith.

Molus denied the premise, but he had previously stated that the conclusion must be accepted.

Calypho said:

"Aye, but you shall not."

He then asked:

"Haven't I touched him, Criticus?"

A touch is a hit in fencing.

"You have both done learnedly," Criticus said, "for as sure as he is a blacksmith, thou are a devil."

"And then he is a devil because he is a blacksmith. Because it was his reason to make me a devil, being a blacksmith," Calypho said.

Molus had previously argued that Vulcan had horns and all men who have horns are devils.

Vulcan is a blacksmith, and he is a devil, and so, according to Calypho, all blacksmiths are devils.

This is Calypho's argument.

Premise 1: Vulcan is a blacksmith.

Premise 2: Vulcan is a devil.

Conclusion: All blacksmiths are devils.

Premise 1: All blacksmiths are devils.

Premise 2: Molus is a blacksmith.

Conclusion: Molus is a devil.

"There is no reasoning with these mechanical dolts, whose wits and intelligence are in their hands, not in their heads," Molus said.

Mechanics are people who work with their hands.

"Don't be angry. You are wise," Criticus said.

But let us conclude this matter as friends with a song."

"I am content," Calypho said. "My voice is as good as my reason."

"Then we have sweet music," Molus said. "But come, I will not break off — I will not fail to keep in time."

They sang a drinking song:

Criticus sang:

"Merry knaves are we three-a,"

Molus sang:

"When our songs do agree-a.

Calypho sang:

"Oh, now I well see-a

"What anon [soon] we shall be-a."

Criticus sang:

"If we ply thus our singing,

Molus sang:

"Pots then must be flinging;"

Calypho sang:

"If the drink be but stinging [pungent],"

Molus sang:

"I shall forget the rules of grammar,

Calypho sang:

"And I the pit-a-pat of my hammer."

All sang:

"To the tap-house [tavern] then let's gang [go] and roar.

"Call hard [call loudly for drinks], 'tis rare [it is splendid] to vamp a score [to run up a bill].

"Draw dry the tub [barrel], be it old or new,

"And part not till the ground look blue."

If the ground looks blue to you, you are very drunk indeed.

All exited.

Phao stood in front of Sybilla's cave.

He said to himself:

"What unfamiliar, strange thoughts are these, Phao, much unfit for thy thoughts: unsuitable for thy working-class birth, thy fortune, thy years, for Phao!

"Unhappy man, can't thou be content to behold the sun without needing to desire to build thy nest in the sun and thy castle in the air?

"Does Sappho bewitch thee, whom all the ladies in Sicily could not woo?"

All the ladies in Sicily were attempting to make Phao fall in love with them, but none was succeeding.

Phao continued:

"Yes, poor Phao, the pride of thy mind is far above the beauty of thy face, and the hardness and cruelty of thy fortune beyond the bitterness of thy words.

"Die, Phao. Phao, die: For there is no hope if thou are wise; nor is there safety if thou are fortunate."

If Phao is wise, he will not woo Sappho and so will miss out on having a relationship with her; if he succeeds in wooing her, he could become the target of envious and malicious factions in the court. (Or a goddess could become jealous.)

Phao continued:

"Ah, Phao, the more thou seek to suppress those growing passions, the loftier they soar, and the more thou wrestle with them, the stronger they grow."

Phao loses whether he struggles against his thoughts of love or he does not struggle against his thoughts of love. If he struggles to suppress his thoughts of love, they fly ever higher. If he does not struggle to suppress his thoughts of love, they grow ever stronger.

Phao continued:

"These thoughts of love are not unlike a ball, which, the harder it is thrown against the earth, the higher it bounces into the air, and they are not unlike our Sicilian stone, which grows hardest by hammering it.

"Oh, divine love! And therefore divine, because love, whose deity no intellectual apprehension can encompass and fully understand, and therefore no authority can constrain him from doing whatever he wants to do; as miraculous in working as he is mighty, and no more to be suppressed than comprehended.

"How are thou now, Phao? To where are thou carried, committing idolatry with that god whom thou have cause to blaspheme?"

Phao was praising a god — the god of love — whom he had reason to curse.

Phao continued:

"Oh, Sappho! Beautiful Sappho!

"Peace! Calm down, miserable wretch, enjoy thy love for Sappho in covert secrecy, wear willow in thy hat, and bays in thy heart."

Willows are a symbol of unrequited love. Wreathes made of laurel (bay) leaves are given to successful poets, athletes, and generals.

Because it was well-known that willows are a symbol of unrequited love, Phao's wearing of willow in his hat would not be "covert secrecy."

Phao continued:

"Lead a lamb in thy hand, and a fox in thy head."

Lambs are known for meekness, and foxes are known for cunning.

Phao continued:

"Have a dove on the back of thy hand, and a sparrow in thy palm."

Doves are the birds of Venus; sparrows are known for lechery.

Phao continued:

"Gold boils best when it bubbles least; water runs smoothest where it is deepest. Let thy love hang at thy heart's bottom — its inmost part, not at the tongue's tip. Things untold are as if they were not done; there can be no greater comfort than to know much, nor is there any less labor than to say nothing.

"But ah, thy beauty, Sappho, thy beauty!

"Do thou, Phao, begin to blab foolishly?

"Aye, blab it, Phao, as long as thou blab copious and true words about her beauty. Bees that die with honey are buried with harmony; swans that end their lives with songs are covered when they are dead with flowers; and they who until their last gasp commend and extol beauty shall be forever honored with benefits.

"In these extremities, I will go to no other oracle than Sybilla, whose old years have not been idle in these young attempts —"

Sappho in her old age was advising the young Phao what to do about his feelings of love.

Phao continued:

"— and whose sound advice may mitigate (although the heavens cannot remove) my miseries.

"Oh, Sappho! Sweet Sappho! Sappho!"

He then called:

"Sybilla."

Sybilla appeared in the mouth of the cave.

"Who is there?" she asked.

"One who is not worthy to be one — that is, not worthy to be alive," Phao said.

"Fair Phao?" Sybilla asked.

"Unfortunate Phao!" he answered.

"Come in," Sybilla said.

Phao said:

"So I will, and I will requite thy tale of Phoebus Apollo with one whose brightness darkens Phoebus the sun-god.

"I love Sappho, Sybilla.

"I love Sappho, ah, Sappho, Sybilla!"

"That is a short tale, Phao, and a sorrowful tale; it asks for pity rather than advice," Sybilla said.

"It is sorrowful, Sybilla: yet in those firm and infirm years of yours, I think there should harbor such experience as may defer for a while, although not take away, my destiny," Phao said.

Old age is debilitating, but it can bring firmness of character and opinion.

"It is hard to cure that by words which cannot be eased by herbal medicines; and yet, if thou will take advice, be attentive," Sybilla said.

"I have brought my ears on purpose, and I will hang at your mouth until you have finished your discourse," Phao said.

Sappho said:

"Love, fair child, is to be governed and managed by art, as thy boat by an oar is governed and managed; for love, although it comes by chance, is ruled by wisdom.

"If my precepts and instructions may persuade thee (and I implore thee, let them persuade thee), I would wish thee first to be diligent and watchful, because women desire nothing more than to have their servants dutiful. Be always in sight, and never be slothful and lazy in showing women affection and attention.

"Flatter — I mean lie. Little things catch light minds, and love is a worm that feeds first upon fennel."

In this society, fennel was associated with flattery.

Sybilla continued:

"Imagine with thyself that all are women to be won; otherwise, my advice would be as unnecessary as thy labor.

"It is impossible for the brittle mettle of women to withstand the flattering attempts of men; only this, let them be asked. Their sex requires no less, and their modesties are to be allowed so much."

In other words: Don't force your attention on women.

Sappho continued:

"Be prodigal and lavish in praises and promises. Beauty must have a trumpet, and pride must have a gift. Peacocks never spread their feathers except when they are flattered, and gods are seldom pleased if they are not bribed with offerings and sacrifices.

"There is no woman so foul — so ugly — who does not think herself fair. In commending, thou cannot lose thy labor, for, by every woman, thou shall be believed.

"Oh, simple women! They are brought rather to believe what their ears hear of flattering men, than what their eyes see in true mirrors!"

"You digress, with the only result being to make me believe that women do so lightly and easily believe," Phao said.

Phao had come here for advice.

Sybilla said:

"Then I will talk to the purpose.

"Choose such times to begin thy suit, as thy lady is in a good humor. The wooden horse entered Troy when the soldiers were quaffing."

Troy fell because of the trick of the Trojan Horse: a large wooden sculpture of a horse. It was hollow and filled with Greek soldiers and left behind when the Greek soldiers appeared to have sailed away from Troy. A lying Greek named

Sinon convinced the Trojans to take the Horse inside the city by saying that according to a prophecy Troy would never fall as long as the Horse was inside the city. That night, the Trojans got drunk, and the Greek soldiers came out of the Horse and went to the gates of Troy, where they let in the Greek soldiers who had sailed back to Troy at night.

The fullest extant account of the fall of Troy is in Book 2 of Virgil's *Aeneid*. Sybilla continued:

"And Penelope, indeed, whom fables make so shy, among the pots wrung her wooers by the fists when she frowned at their faces."

In Homer's *Odyssey*, Penelope was a faithful wife throughout the twenty years her husband Ulysses (his Greek name is Odysseus) was away from home. The first ten years he spent fighting the Trojan War, and the second ten years he spent trying to get back home. Much of that time he was kept captive on an island by the goddess Calypso.

During much of that time, people assumed that Ulysses was dead, and over 100 suitors tried to convince Penelope to marry one of them. Penelope was able to hold them off for some time with her famous weaving trick. She told them that after she had woven a shroud for Ulysses' father, Laertes, she would choose one of them to marry. Each day she wove the shroud, and each night she unwove what she had woven.

But according to Sybilla, although Penelope presented a chaste face to the public, when she was drunk among the pots of liquids containing alcohol, she secretly squeezed the hands of the suitors.

Sybilla continued:

"Grapes are mind-glasses."

Drunk people say what is on their mind.

Sybilla continued:

"Venus works in Bacchus' wine press, and she blows fire upon his liquor.

"When thou talk with her — Sappho — let thy speech be pleasant and amusing, but not exaggerated and not to be believed. Choose such words as may (as many may) melt her mind and lower her resistance. Honey rankles when it is eaten for pleasure, and fair words wound when they are heard instead of love."

In other words: Be careful not to overdo your wooing.

Sybilla continued:

"Write, and persist in writing: They read more into what is written to them than is in fact written to them, and write less than they think.

"When being witty, strive to be pleasant; in attire strive to be well-dressed, but not too extravagant.

"When she smiles, laugh outright; if she rises, stand up; if she sits, lie down.

"Use all thy time to keep time with her and keep her pace.

"Can you sing? Then show your ability.

"Can you dance? Then use your legs.

"Can you play upon any instrument? Then practice your fingers to please her fancy.

"Seek out qualities and skills that you can display.

"If she seems at first to be cruel, don't be discouraged. I tell thee a strange thing: Women strive because they would be overcome.

"'Force' they call it, but they account it such a welcome force that they continually make it their aim to be overcome."

Such "force" is seduction, not rape.

Some women play hard to get, not impossible to get.

Sybilla continued:

"To fair words join sweet kisses, which if they gently and tenderly receive — I say no more, they will gently receive."

"I say no more."

In gestures: Nudge, nudge. Wink, wink.

Seduction can be effective.

Sybilla continued:

"But don't be pinned always on her sleeves: Strangers have green rushes, when daily guests are not worth a rush."

Rushes were strewn on floors. When an important visitor was coming, fresh, green rushes replaced the old rushes.

"Not worth a rush" means "worthless."

Sybilla continued:

"Look pale, and learn to be lean, so that whoever sees thee may say, 'The gentleman is in love.'

"Use no sorcery to hasten thy success: Wit is a witch.

"Ulysses was not fair, but he was wise; he was not cunning in charms, but he was sweet in speech. His filed — polished and smooth — tongue made those enamored who sought to have enchanted him."

Ulysses was a master of rhetoric. At one point in his travels, he and his men stayed with the enchantress Circe, who loved him. When they were ready to go, Ulysses had to convince Circe to allow them to leave. When telling his tale to other people during his travels, he said:

"That night I entreated Circe to let us go. I did not want to make her angry, so I made it clear that my men were the ones who were restless and wanted to leave, but I also said that I, too, longed for my homecoming."

Similarly, when another goddess, Calypso, wanted Ulysses to stay with her, Ulysses told her:

"Don't be angry with me, please. I know that you speak the truth. My wife is not as beautiful as you. My wife's figure is not better than yours. How can a mortal woman compare to an immortal goddess? The immortal goddess will always be more beautiful.

"But I want to see my home again. I want to see Ithaca again. That is what I have been longing for every day. I have faced many troubles before, and I am willing to face more troubles if only I can see my home again."

Ulysses could have each goddess that he missed his wife, Penelope, and he wanted to see her again, but Circe and Calypso each could have seen that as a rejection of her charms. Each goddess could have thought that Ulysses loved Penelope and that he did not love her. Angry gods and goddesses can do horrible things to human beings, as Diana did when Actaeon, a hunter, accidentally saw her bathing naked. She turned him into a stag, and his own hunting hounds killed him.

But Ulysses wanted to see his home again? That was a good reason to leave, although each goddess preferred that he stay with her.

Ulysses was a man of action, but he could show great sensitivity. After he returned to Ithaca and reestablished himself as its king, he did not immediately jump into bed with Penelope; instead, first he talked to her and he proved to her that he was her long-lost husband without room for doubt.

Sybilla continued:

"Don't be coy: Don't be either shy or hard to get.

"Bear with her and soothe and cajole her and bear gifts to her, swear, die to please thy lady.

"These are rules for poor lovers; to others I am no mistress."

This kind of mistress is a mentor.

Sybilla continued:

"He has wit enough, who can give enough."

A proverb stated, "He is wise who is rich."

Sybilla continued:

"Dumb men are eloquent if they are liberal in bestowing gifts. Believe me, great gifts are little gods."

A rich man who gives valuable gifts to women will not lack girlfriends.

Sybilla continued:

"When thy mistress bends her brow and frowns, do not bend thy fist and make a threatening gesture. Cammocks must be bowed with sleight, not strength."

Cammocks are trees that can be trained to grow in various shapes. When trained properly, their branches can make good canes.

Sybilla continued:

"Water is to be trained — that is, conducted — with pipes, not stopped with sluices and dams; fire is to be quenched with dust, not with swords.

"If thou have a rival, be patient."

Ovid, *Ars Amatoria* (*The Art of Love*), Book 2, lines 539-540, states, "*Rivalem patienter habe. Victoria tecum / Stabit.*"

Translated, the quotation says, "Be patient with your rival. Victory rests with you."

Sybilla continued:

"Art, not malice, must draw thy rival out of the way; time, not might and force, must draw thy rival out of the way; her change from loving him to loving thee, and thy constancy, must draw thy rival out of the way.

"Whatsoever she wears, swear it becomes her.

"In thy love be secret. Venus' coffers, although they are hollow, never sound, and when they seem emptiest, they are fullest."

True: A lover's coffers may be hollow, but they ought not to sound hollow when they are thumped because they are full.

Also true: A lover's coffers should be emptied in order in order to buy gifts for the beloved.

In other words: Wooing is expensive. A lover's coffers have to be constantly replenished in order to spend even more to buy gifts for the beloved.

One wonders about some of Sybilla's advice. Does it have the same acumen as the reasoning about the devil displayed earlier?

But this is possibly true: A mean between extremes is best. Keep the coffers half-full.

Some of Sybilla's advice seems contradictory:

• "Be always in sight, and never be slothful and lazy in showing women affection and attention."

• "But don't be pinned always on her sleeves: Strangers have green rushes, when daily guests are not worth a rush."

Sybilla continued:

"Old fool that I am! To do thee good, I begin to dote and act foolishly, and counsel that which I would have concealed."

She had revealed to Phao some women's secrets.

Sybilla continued:

"Thus, Phao, I have given thee certain ways of regarding your situation, no rules, only to set thee on your way, not to bring thee home."

Sybilla had provided guidelines, not rules.

Phao said, "Ah, Sybilla, I ask you to continue giving me advice, so that I may glut myself in this knowledge."

Sybilla said:

"Thou shall not surfeit and overeat, Phao, while I provide thy diet.

"Flies that die on the honeysuckle become poison to bees.

"A little advice in love is a great deal."

"But all that can be said is not enough," Phao said.

"White silver draws black lines, and sweet words will breed sharp torments," Sybilla said.

"What shall become of me?" Phao asked.

"Go dare," Sybilla said. "Be brave and act and find out what will become of you."

Sybilla exited into her cave.

Phao said:

"I go now!"

He then said to himself:

"Phao, thou can only die — you have no choice to do otherwise — and so then it is as good to die with great desires, as it is to pine in base fortunes."

CHAPTER 3

— 3.1 —

In the anteroom of Sappho's chamber, Trachinus the courier, Pandion the scholar, Mileta, Ismena, Criticus, and Molus met. Sappho was ill and was in her chamber. Mileta and Ismena were court ladies.

"Sappho has fallen suddenly sick," Trachinus said. "I cannot guess the cause."

"Some cold, likely, or else a woman's qualm such as a fainting fit or nausea," Mileta said.

"A strange nature of cold, to drive one into such a heat and fever," Pandion said.

"Your medical skill, sir, I think is of the second place, not the first," Mileta said, "else you would not judge it rare that hot fevers are engendered by cold causes."

Catching a cold can lead to a fever. Also, pursuing a cold loved one may inflame passion.

"Indeed, lady, I have no more medical skill than will purge choler; and that if it pleases you, I will practice upon you," Pandion said. "It is good for women who are waspish."

"Choler" is anger. Pandion claims to know how to make someone's temperament calm, although his calling a woman waspish is unlikely to do that. A waspish woman is irritable and spiteful.

"Indeed, sir, no," Ismena said. "You had best purge your own melancholy. It is likely that you are a male-content."

"It is true, and aren't you a female-content?" Pandion asked.

"Quiet!" Trachinus said. "I am not content that a male-content and a female-content should go together."

He thought that a male-content and a female-content — malcontents of each sex — ought not to be a couple.

"Ismena is disposed to be merry," Mileta said.

"No, it is Pandion who is eager to seem wise," Ismena said.

"You shall not fall out and argue," Trachinus said, "for pigeons, after biting, fall to billing, and open jars make the closest jests."

"Billing" is avian kissing: cooing bill to bill. Pigeons that coo together, stay together.

"Jars" are quarrels, and "closest" is most secret and hidden.

Lots of couples quarrel loudly and then have make-up sex.

Eugenua, another court lady, entered the scene.

She said, "Mileta! Ismena! Mileta! Come away! My lady is in a swoon!"

Sappho had fainted.

"Aye me! I am woeful," Mileta said.

"Come, let's hurry," Ismena said.

Eugenua, Mileta, and Ismena exited.

"I am sorry for Sappho because she will take no medicine," Trachinus said. "She is like you, Pandion, who, being sick with the sullens, will seek no friend."

The sullens is a case of melancholy or depression, and in this context, "friend" means "medicinal remedy."

"From men we learn to speak, from gods we learn to hold our peace," Pandion said. "Silence shall digest what folly has swallowed, and wisdom shall wean what fancy has nursed."

In other words: People sometimes have foolish and fanciful ideas that calm consideration can correct.

"Isn't it love?" Trachinus asked.

He thought that Sappho was in love.

"If it were, what then?" Pandion said.

"Nothing, but that I hope it is not love," Trachinus said.

Pandion said:

"Why, in courts there is nothing more common.

"To be bald among the Micanians was accounted no shame because they were all bald; and so, to be in love among courtiers is no discredit because they are all in love."

The Micanians are the people of the Greek island named Myconos. Pliny wrote a book in which he stated that all the people there were born bald.

"Why, what do you think of our ladies?" Trachinus asked.

"The same as I think about the Seres wool, which being the whitest and softest, frets the soonest and deepest," Pandion said.

The word "frets" can mean 1) wears away, or 2) fusses and complains.

"I will not tempt you in your deep melancholy, lest you seem sour to those — the ladies — who are so sweet," Trachinus said. "But come, let us walk a little into the fields. It may be the open air will disclose your close conceits."

"Close conceits" are "secret opinions."

"I will go with you, but let's send our pages away," Pandion said.

Trachinus and Pandion exited, leaving their pages — Criticus and Molus — behind.

"What brown study are thou in, Molus?" Criticus asked. "No mirth? No life?"

A brown study is a state of gloomy musing.

"I am in the depth of my learning driven to a musing state as I wonder how this Lent I shall scamble — make shift — in the court, I who was accustomed to fast so often in the university," Molus said.

Lent is a period of fasting.

"Thy belly is thy god," Criticus said.

"Then he is a deaf god," Molus said.

"Why?" Criticus asked.

Molus said:

"For *venter non habet aures.*"

The Latin means, "The belly has no ears."

In other words: Talk about food will not make the belly less empty.

Molus continued:

"But thy back is thy god."

Criticus wore fine clothing on his back.

"Then it is a blind god," Criticus said.

"How can you prove that?" Molus asked.

"Easy," Criticus said. "*Nemo videt manticae quod in tergo est.*"

The Latin means, "No one sees the satchel on his own back."

A fable told about a man who carried a satchel of other people's faults in his arms and carried a satchel of his own faults in a bag on his back. The man could easily see other people's faults, but he could not see his own faults.

"Then I wish that the satchel that hangs at your god, *id est*, your back, were full of food to stuff my god, *hoc est*, my belly," Molus said.

Both Latin phrases mean, "That is."

"Excellent," Criticus said. "But how can thou study, when thy mind is only in the kitchen?"

"Doesn't the horse travel best that sleeps with its head in the manger?" Molus asked.

Well-fed horses travel best.

"Yes, but what then?" Criticus said.

"Good wits will apply," Molus replied.

In other words: An intelligent man will find a way to interpret a saying to make a point in his favor.

Molus then asked:

"But what cheer is there here this Lent?"

"Cheer" is food and drink.

"Fish," Criticus said.

"I can eat none," Molus said. "It is wind."

"Wind" is air.

According to Molus, fish is light food that does not fill him up the way that heavier food such as meat would.

"Eggs," Criticus said.

"I must eat none, they are fire," Molus said.

Possibly, eggs gave him heartburn. Or fiery farts.

"Cheese," Criticus said.

"It is against the old verse, *caseus est nequam*," Molus said.

The Latin means, "Cheese is nothing."

"Yea, but it digests all things except itself," Criticus said.

Many people in this society held the belief that cheese was indigestible but helped the stomach to digest other food.

"Yes, but if a man has nothing else to eat, what shall it digest?" Molus asked.

"You are disposed to jest," Criticus said. "But if your silken throat can swallow no packthread, you must pick your teeth, and play with your trencher."

Unless Molus' fastidious throat can swallow common food during Lent, Molus will have to pick his teeth with a toothpick and play with his plate — and fast, which is what Lent is all about.

Molus said:

"So shall I not incur the fulsome and unmannerly — the reprehensible — sin of surfeiting, aka eating too much."

Gluttony is one of the seven deadly sins.

Molus then said:

"But here comes Calypho."

Calypho the Cyclops entered the scene.

"What is the news?" Criticus asked.

"Since I was last here, I have sweat like a dog to prove my master is a devil," Calypho said. "He brought such reasons to refel" — he meant "repel," aka "refute" — "me as, I promise and assure you, I shall think the better of his wit, as long as I am with him."

Vulcan had a good intelligence and could argue well.

"How did he refute your arguments?" Molus asked.

Calypho replied:

"Like this.

"I was always arguing that he had horns, and therefore he was a devil, but he said, 'Fool, they are things like horns, but no horns. For once a solemn session was being held in the assembly of gods, and in the midst of their talk, I put in my sentence, aka judgment or opinion, which was so indifferent that they all concluded it might as well have been left out as put in, and so they placed on each side of my head things like horns and called me a *parenthesis.*'

"Now, my masters, this may be true, for I have seen it (a set of parentheses) myself in various sentences."

Indeed, parentheses can look like horns. Imagine them on the sides of the forehead with a pair of eyes between their bottoms:

(..)

"It is true, and the same did Mars make a full point, so that Vulcan's head was made a *parenthesis*," Molus said.

A full point can be 1) a full stop, aka period, or 2) a full erection.

Parentheses resemble horns, and by cuckolding Vulcan, Mars gave him a pair of parentheses.

"This shall go with me," Criticus said. "I will remember it. I trust in Syracuse to give one or other man a *parenthesis.*"

Criticus wanted to cuckold one or more husbands.

By cuckolding one or more husbands, Criticus could be giving them a parent-thesis. A thesis is a topic for discussion, and people, including the husband, could discuss whether the husband or Criticus was the real father of a child.

"Has Venus yet come home?" Molus asked.

Calypho said, "No, but if I were Vulcan, I would by the gods —"

"What would thou do?" Criticus asked.

"Nothing, but like Vulcan, I would halt by the gods," Calypho said.

"Halt" can mean 1) limp, or 2) stop speaking (when he was around the gods).

"I thought you would have hardly entreated Venus," Criticus said.

"Hardly entreated" can mean 1) "little begged," 2) "vigorously begged," or 3) "begged with difficulty."

"Nay, Venus is easily entreated; but let that go by," Calypho said.

"Let what go by?" Criticus asked.

"That which makes so many *parenthesis*," Calypho said.

In other words: Let's stop discussing this topic of cuckoldry.

"I must go by — leave — too, or else my master will not go by me, but will meet me full with his fist and thrash me," Molus said. "Therefore, if we shall sing, give me my part quickly, for if I tarry long, I shall cry my part woefully and lament my lot in life.

They sang a drinking song:

All sang:

"*Arm, arm, the foe comes on apace [quickly].*"

Calypho sang:

"*What's that red nose and sulfury [fiery] face?*"

Molus sang:

"*'Tis [It is] the hot leader.*"

Criticus sang:

"*What's his name?*"

Molus sang:

"*Bacchus, a captain of plump fame [great reputation]:*

"*A goat [is] the beast on which he rides,*

"*Fat grunting swine run by his sides,*

"*His standard-bearer [flag-holder] fears no knocks,*

"*For he's a drunken butter-box,*

"*Who when i' th' red field [bloody battlefield] thus he revels,*

"*Cries out, 'ten tousan ton of tevils!'*" [Stereotypical Dutch dialect: The Dutch had a reputation for loving butter and were called butter-boxes.]"

Calypho sang:

"*What's he [Who is he who] so swaggers in the van [vanguard, front of the army]?*"

Molus sang:

"Oh! that's a roaring Englishman,

"Who in deep healths [deeply drunk toasts] does so excel,

"From Dutch and French he bears the bell [wins first place]."

Criticus sang:

"What vict'lers [vitualers: people who supply food and other provisions] follow Bacchus' camps?"

Molus sang:

"Fools, fiddlers, panders, pimps, and ramps [wanton women]."

Calypho sang:

"See, see, the battle now grows hot;

"Here legs fly [legs are blown off on the battlefield, or drinkers' legs collapse], here goes heads to the pot [to ruin, or to the drinking pot],

"Here whores and knaves toss broken glasses,

"Here all the soldiers look like asses."

Criticus sang:

"What man ever heard such hideous noise?"

Molus sang:

"That's the vintner's bawling boys. Anon, anon, [Soon, soon] the trumpets are,

"Which call them to the fearful bar."

Calypho sang:

"Rush in, and let's our forces try."

Molus sang:

"Oh, no, for see they fly [flee], they fly [flee]!"

Criticus sang:

"And so will I."

Calypho sang:

"And I."

Molus sang:

"And I."

All sang:

"'Tis [It is] a hot day in drink to die."

They exited.

In her chamber, Sappho was lying in her bed. Some visitors arrived: the court ladies Mileta, Ismena, Canope, Eugenua, Favilla, and Lamia.

Sappho sighed and said, "I don't know which way to turn myself. Ah, ah, I faint, I die."

"Madam, I think it would be good if you were to put on more bedclothes and sweat it out," Mileta said.

"No, no, the best relief I find is to sigh it out," Sappho said.

"It is a strange disease that would breed such a desire," Ismena said.

"It is a strange desire that has brought such a disease," Sappho said.

Her desire for Phao had caused her love sickness.

The court ladies thought that her illness was physical, not emotional.

"Where, Lady, do you feel your most pain?" Canope asked.

"Where nobody else can feel it, Canope," Sappho answered.

"At the heart?" Canope asked.

"In the heart," Sappho answered.

"At the heart" is a physical ailment; "in the heart" is a love ailment.

"Will you have any mithridate?" Canope asked.

Mithridate was an antidote for poison.

"Yes, if for this disease there were any mithridate," Sappho said.

"Why? What disease is it, madam, that medicine cannot cure?" Mileta asked.

"Only the disease, Mileta, that I have," Sappho said.

"Is it a burning ague — a fever?" Mileta asked.

"I think so, or a burning agony," Sappho answered.

"Will you have any of this syrup to moisten your mouth?" Eugenua asked.

"I wish I had some local things to dry my brain," Sappho said.

"Local things" are medicines that treat one part of the body.

In this society, moist palms were a sign of lechery, and a "thing" could be a penis.

If Sappho could sleep with Phao, her lechery would be satisfied, and her brain would be dry.

"Madam, will you see if you can sleep?" Favilla asked.

"Sleep, Favilla? I shall then dream," Sappho said.

"It is as good to dream while asleep, as it is to sigh while awake," Lamia said.

"Phao is cunning and skilled in all kinds of simples, and it is unlikely that there is none to procure sleep," Eugenua said.

"Simples" are herbal medicines.

"Who?" Sappho asked.

"Phao," Eugenua answered.

Sappho said:

"Yes, Phao! Phao!

"Ah, Phao, let him come immediately!"

"Shall we draw the curtains while you give yourself to slumber and fall asleep?" Mileta asked.

Sappho said:

"Do, but don't depart. I have such starts in my sleep, which is disquieted I don't know how or why."

Slumbering, she said:

"Phao! Phao!"

"What do you say, madam?" Ismena asked.

Sappho said:

"Nothing, but if I don't sleep now, you send for Phao.

"Ah, gods!"

Sappho fell asleep, and her attendants drew the curtains around her bed.

"There is a fish called garus, that heals all sickness, as long as while it is applied no one says its name: garus," Mileta said.

"That is an evil medicine for us women, for if we should be forbidden to say the name 'garus,' we should chat nothing but 'garus,'" Eugenua said.

The name that Sappho should not say is Phao.

Combine "Phao" with "garus," and the result is "Phaogarus."

"—phagous" is used in combination with other words. It means "feeding on" the word it is combined with. For example, "ichthyophagous" means "feeding on fish."

"—phagous" is derived from the Greek word *phagein*, which means "to eat, to devour."

Sappho was saying the name "Phao" often.

In this case, "—phagous" was combined with nothing, and Sappho's body was feeding on itself: She was wasting away.

If Sappho could sexually "feed" on Phao, her illness would disappear.

"Well said, Eugenua, you know yourself," Canope said.

"Know thyself" was a saying found at Delphi, where was the Delphic Oracle.

"Yes, Canope, and you know that I am one of your sex," Eugenua said.

As women, they shared some of the same faults.

"I have heard of an herb called lunary [moonwort, a fern], that being bound to the pulses of the sick, causes nothing but dreams of weddings and dances," Ismena said.

"I think, Ismena, that herb is at thy pulses now for thou are always talking of romantic matchings and merriments," Favilla said.

"It is an unlucky sign in the chamber of the sick to talk of marriages, for my mother said it predicts death," Canope said.

"It is very evil, too, Canope, to sit at the bed's feet, and it predicts danger; therefore, move your stool, and sit by me," Mileta said.

Canope moved and sat by Mileta.

"Surely, she has taken some cold," Lamia said.

"If someone were burnt to death, I think we women would say that he died of a cold," Ismena said.

"It may be some conceit," Favilla said.

In this context, a conceit is a psychosomatic illness.

"Then there is no fear, for I never did hear yet of a woman who died of a conceit," Mileta said.

"I don't fear that she will die, for the owl has not shrieked at the window, nor has the night raven croaked, both of which signs are fatal and ominous," Eugenua said.

"Fatal" means "ominous."

"You are all superstitious, for these are only fancies of doting old age, who by chance observing it in some, have set it down as a religion for all," Favilla said.

This is how some superstitions start. One thing happens, then another thing happens. Someone erroneously thinks the first thing caused the second thing.

For example, a black cat crossed my path and then I had bad luck. I conclude that if a black cat crosses your path, you can expect to have bad luck.

"Favilla, thou are only a girl," Mileta said. "I would not have a weasel cry, nor desire to look into a mirror, nor an old wife come into my chamber; for then, although I lingered in my disease, I should never escape it."

Apparently, these are things that Mileta associates with bad luck. Weasels are bad-luck animals (some hunters in this society believed that if you see a weasel in the morning, you will have bad luck all day), mirrors can be dropped and broken (or can show an ill face), and old ladies may be witches.

Mileta was superstitious. She wished to avoid signs of bad luck.

Sappho asked:

"Ah, who is there?"

The bedcurtains were drawn back.

Sappho then said:

"What sudden frights are these? I thought that Phao came with simples to make me sleep. Did nobody name Phao before I began to slumber?"

"Yes, we told you about him," Mileta said.

"Let him be here tomorrow," Sappho said.

"He shall," Mileta said. "Will you have a little broth to comfort you?"

"I can relish and enjoy no food," Sappho said.

"Yet you must eat a little food to sustain nature," Mileta said.

Sappho said:

"I cannot, Mileta. I will not.

"Oh, which way shall I lie? What shall I do?"

She sighed and then said:

"Oh, Mileta, help to raise me up in my bed; my head lies too low. You pester me with too many bedclothes. Bah, you keep the chamber too hot — leave my chamber.

"It may be I shall steal a nap when all of you are gone."

"We will," Mileta said.

All the court ladies exited.

Alone, Sappho said to herself:

"Ah, impatient, restless disease of love, and goddess of love thrice unmerciful. The eagle is never stricken with thunder, nor the olive with lightning; and may great ladies be plagued with love?"

If great things such as eagles (king of birds, associated with Jupiter, king of the gods) and olive trees (associated with Minerva, goddess of wisdom) enjoy protection, why not Sappho, princess of Syracuse)?

Sappho continued talking to herself:

"Oh, Venus, haven't I strewn thine altars with sweet roses? Haven't I kept thy swans in clear rivers? Haven't I fed thy sparrows with ripe corn? And haven't I harbored thy doves in fair houses?"

Swans, doves, and sparrows are all associated with Venus. Swans pull her chariot in the sky. Turtledoves are symbols of loyalty in love matches. In this society, sparrows were associated with lechery.

Sappho continued talking to herself:

"Thy tortoise I have nourished under my fig tree, I have decorated the ceiling of my bedchamber with thy cockleshells, and I have dipped thy sponge into the freshest waters."

Venus appeared with a sponge in a painting by the 4th-century B.C.E. Greek artist Protogenes, and she appeared standing on a cockleshell in a painting by Botticelli.

Occasionally, she has been depicted with one foot on a tortoise. Tortoises are associated with staying at home because they carry their homes on their back. Figs have been associated with female genitalia.

Sappho continued talking to herself:

"Did thou nurse me in my swaddling clothes with wholesome herbs, just so that I might perish in my flowering years — the prime years of my life — from love?

"I perceive, but too late I perceive, and yet not too late, because at last, that strains are caught as well by stooping too low, as by reaching too high; that eyes are bleared as soon with vapors that come from the earth, as with beams that proceed from the sun. Love lodges sometimes in caves; and thou, Phoebus Apollo, that in the pride of thy heat shines all day in our horizon, at night dips thy head in the ocean."

Phao was from a lower social class than Sappho's, and yet she had fallen in love with him.

Sappho was from a higher social class than Phao's, and yet he had fallen in love with her.

Sappho continued talking to herself:

"Resist it, Sappho, while love is yet tender and young.

"From acorns come oaks, from drops come floods, from sparks come flames, and from atoms come elements."

Resisting something small early may keep it from becoming big.

Sappho continued talking to herself:

"But alas, it fares with me as with wasps, who, feeding on serpents, make their stings more venomous: By glutting myself on the face of Phao, I have made my desire more desperate.

"Into the nest of a halcyon [the kingfisher], no bird can enter except the halcyon; and into the heart of so great a lady, can anyone creep except a great lord?

"There is an herb (not unlike unto my love), which, the further it grows from the sea, the saltier it is; and my desires, the more they swerve from reason, the more they seem reasonable and rational.

"When Phao comes, what then? Will thou open and reveal thy love?

"Yes.

"No, Sappho, but staring in his face until thine eyes dazzle, and thy spirits faint, I will die before his face.

"Then this shall be written on thy tomb:

"'Though thy love were greater than wisdom could endure, yet thine honor was such as love could not violate.'"

She then called, "Mileta!"

Mileta and Ismena entered Sappho's bed-chamber.

"I come," Mileta said.

"Peace will not happen," Sappho said. "I can take no rest, whichever way I turn."

"This is a strange malady!" Mileta said.

Sappho said:

"Mileta, if thou don't mind, it is a strange martyrdom."

Martyrdoms involve intense suffering. Sappho was a martyr for love.

Sappho continued:

"But give me my lute, and I will see if in song I can beguile my own eyes and deceive them into falling asleep."

Mileta got the lute, handed it to Sappho, and said, "Here, madam."

"Have you sent for Phao?" Sappho asked.

"Yes," Mileta answered.

"And you told him to bring simples that will procure sleep?" Sappho asked.

"No," Mileta said.

Sappho said:

"Foolish wench, what should the boy do here, if he doesn't bring any remedies with him? Do you think that perhaps I could sleep if I did just see him?

"Let him not come at all — yes, let him come — no, it doesn't matter. Yet I will try, let him come."

These days, "come" is sometimes spelled "cum."

Sappho continued:

"Do you hear me?"

"Yes, madam, it shall be done," Mileta said.

She left the bedchamber and then said to Ismena, "Peace, no noise. She begins to fall asleep. I will go to Phao."

Ismena replied:

"Go speedily, for if she wakes up and does not find you here, she will be angry.

"Sick folks are testy, who although they eat nothing, yet they feed on gall."

Irritable people figuratively feed on gall, aka bile, a secretion of the liver.

Mileta exited, while Ismena withdrew.

Sappho sang:

"*Oh, cruel Love [Cupid]! on thee I lay*

"*My curse, which shall strike blind the day:*"

Her curse will make him blind.

Sappho continued with her curse:

"*Never may sleep with velvet hand*

"*Charm thine eyes with sacred wand;*

"*Thy jailers shall be hopes and fears;*

"*Thy prison-mates, [Thy prison-mates shall be] groans, sighs, and tears;*

"*Thy play, [Thy pastime shall be] to wear out weary times,*

"*Fantastic passions, vows, and rhymes;*

"*Thy bread [shall] be frowns, thy drink [shall] be gall,*

"*Such as when you Phao call.*

"The bed thou liest on [shall] be despair;

"Thy sleep, [Thy sleep shall be] fond [mad] dreams; thy dreams, [dreams shall be] long care;

"Hope (like thy fool [jester]) at thy bed's head,

"Mock [Shall mock] thee, till madness strike thee dead,

"As [Just as] Phao, thou dost me [thou strike me dead] with thy proud eyes;

"In thee poor Sappho lives; for thee she dies."

In the ante-room to Sappho's chamber, Mileta and Phao talked.

"I wish that either your cunning, Phao, or your fortune and luck might by simples — herbal remedies — provoke my lady to some slumber," Mileta said.

"My simples are in their operation like my simplicity is, which if they do little good, assuredly they can do no harm," Phao said.

His "simplicity" was his foolishness. He was saying that he was just a simple man.

Physicians follow (or try to follow) this guideline: Do no harm.

"If I were sick, the very sight of thy fair face would drive me into a sound sleep," Mileta said.

Hmm. Mileta has fallen in love with Phao.

"Indeed, gentlewomen are so drowsy in their desires, that they can scarcely hold up their eyes for love," Phao said.

Women's "bedroom eyes" can be languorous.

Mileta explained what she had meant: "I mean the delight of beauty would so bind and blind my senses that I would be quickly rocked into a deep rest."

"You women have an excuse for an advantage, which must be allowed, because only to you women it was allotted," Phao said.

Women have an advantage because they are women; men will sometimes allow them to win arguments without much argument because they are women.

Mileta said:

"Phao, thou are surpassingly good-looking, and thou are able to draw and attract a chaste eye, not only to glance, but to gaze on thee.

"Thy young years, thy quick wit, thy stayed and staid desires are of force to control and overmaster those who should command."

"Stayed" desires are suppressed desires. Phao was able to control his sexual desires even when an upper-class woman such as Mileta (or Sappho) was attracted to him.

"Staid" desires are steadfast desires.

Mileta was of a higher social class than Phao, and she was the one to command. She was doing the chasing, not Phao.

Phao realized that he had committed a faux pas by not praising Mileta's beauty.

He said, "Lady, I forgot to commend you first, and lest I should have overslipped — failed — to praise you at all, you have brought in my beauty, which is simple and unadorned, so that in courtesy I might remember yours, which is singular and without peer."

His words can be interpreted as saying that Mileta was fishing for compliments.

"You mistake my words on purpose, and deliberately misconstrue my words out of malice," Mileta said.

"I am as far from malice as you from love, and to mistake your words on purpose would be to mislike you out of peevish foolishness," Phao said.

Phao's saying that Mileta was far from love meant only that she was far from loving *him*, but she misunderstood it as saying that she was incapable of loving anyone.

"As far as I from love? Why, do you think that I am so dull that I cannot love, or so spiteful that I will not love?" Mileta asked.

"Neither, lady, but how should men imagine women can love, when in their mouths there is nothing rifer — more commonly spoken — than 'Truly, I do not love,'" Phao said.

"Why, will you have women's love in their tongues?" Mileta asked. "Do you want women to openly reveal their hearts?"

"Yes, else I think there is no love in their hearts," Phao said.

"Why?" Mileta asked.

"Because there was never anything in the bottom of a woman's heart that does not come to her tongue's end," Phao said.

A proverb stated, "Trust a secret with no woman," aka "Entrust no secret to a woman."

Phao was making an argument:

Premise 1: Women always reveal what is in their heart.

Premise 2: If a woman does love a man, she will reveal that love.

Premise 3: A woman does not reveal that she loves a man.

Conclusion: That woman does not love that man.

"You are too young to cheapen and trivialize love," Mileta said.

"Yet I am old enough to talk with market folks," Phao said.

He was interpreting the word "cheapen" to mean "haggle and attempt to get a lower price for an item one is buying."

"Well, let us go in," Mileta said.

Some curtains were drawn back, revealing Ismena and Sappho.

"Phao has come," Ismena said.

"Who? Phao?" Sappho asked. "Phao, let him come near, but who sent for him?"

"You did, madam," Mileta said.

Sappho said:

"I am loath to take any medicines, yet I must, rather than pine in these maladies."

"Pine" can mean wasting away because of lovesickness.

Sappho continued:

"Phao, you may make me sleep, if you will."

"If I can, I must, if you want me to," Phao replied.

"What herbs have you brought, Phao?" Sappho asked.

"Such as will make you sleep, madam, although they cannot make me slumber," Phao replied.

"Why, how can you cure me, when you cannot remedy yourself?" Sappho asked.

Phao said, "Yes, madam, the causes of my insomnia and your insomnia are contrary, for it is only a dryness in your brains that keeps you from rest, but —"

Previously, Sappho had wanted something to dry her brain.

"— but what?" Sappho interrupted.

"Nothing, but mine is not so," Phao said.

His brain was wet. In this society, a moist palm was a sign of lechery, although Phao's wet brain was due to love.

Phao was assuming that Sappho's illness was physical, while his was emotional.

"Nay, then I despair of help if our diseases are not all one," Sappho said.

She wanted both Phao and her to be suffering from lovesickness.

"I wish our diseases were all one and the same," Phao said.

In fact, they were all one and the same: lovesickness.

"It goes hard with the patient, when the physician is desperate," Sappho said.

The physician, Phao, was desperately in love, but by "desperate," Sappho meant "unable to cure his patient."

"Yet Medea made the ever-waking dragon to snort and snore, when she, poor soul, could not close her eyes and sleep," Phao said.

"Medea was in love, and nothing could cause her rest but Jason," Sappho said.

In Apollonius of Rhodes' *Argonautica*, Jason traveled in search of the Golden Fleece. A young woman, Medea, who was skilled in herbs, fell in love with him and could not sleep. She helped him to get the golden fleece by putting to sleep the huge always-awake dragon (or snake) guarding it.

Phao said, "Indeed, I know no herb to make lovers sleep, except heartsease, which, because it grows so high, I cannot reach, for —"

"For whom?" Sappho asked.

"For such as love," Phao said.

Sappho said, "It grows very low, and I can never stoop to it, so that —"

"That what?" Phao asked.

Sappho said:

"So that I may gather it."

Heartsease is a name given to two plants. One grows very high (the wallflower, which climbs upward on walls), and the other grows very low (the pansy).

Sappho's social position is very high, and Phao's social position is very low.

Sappho then asked:

"But why do you sigh so, Phao?"

"It is my custom, madam," Phao said.

"It will do you harm, and me, too," Sappho said, "for I never hear someone sigh, but I must sigh, also."

A folk belief alleged that one sigh resulted in the loss of one drop of blood from the heart.

"It would be best, then, that your ladyship would give me leave — permission — to be gone, for I can only sigh," Phao said.

Sappho said:

"Nay, stay, for now I begin to sigh, I shall not leave — stop — although you would be gone.

"But what do you think best for your sighing to take it away?"

"Yew, madam," Phao said.

"Yew" is a tree. "Yew" is pronounced like "you."

"Me?" Sappho said.

"No, madam, yew of the tree," Phao said.

"Then I will love yew the better. And, indeed, I think it would make me sleep, too; therefore, all other simples set aside, I will simply use only yew," Sappho said.

"Do, madam, for I think nothing in the world is as good as yew," Phao said.

"Farewell for this time," Sappho said.

Phao went into the anteroom just as Venus and Cupid entered it.

Venus asked him, "Isn't your name Phao?"

"I am Phao, fair Venus, whom you made so good-looking," Phao said.

Venus said, "So surpassingly good-looking! Oh, fair Phao. Oh, sweet Phao. What will thou do for Venus?"

Hmm. Venus has fallen in love with Phao.

"Anything that comes in the compass — within the limit — of my poor fortune," Phao answered.

"Cupid shall teach thee to shoot, and I will instruct thee in how to dissemble," Venus said.

"I will learn anything but dissembling," Phao said.

"Why, my boy?" Venus asked.

"Because then I must learn to be a woman," Phao said.

"Thou heard that from a man," Venus said.

"Men speak truth," Phao said.

He must have heard that from a man, too.

"But truth is a she, and truth is so always painted — depicted," Venus said.

"I think a painted — pretended — truth," Phao said.

"Well, farewell for this time, for I must visit Sappho," Venus said.

Phao exited.

CHAPTER 4

— 4.1 —

Venus and Cupid visited Sappho in her bedchamber.

"Sappho, I have heard thy complaints, and pitied thine agonies," Venus said.

Sappho said:

"Oh, Venus, my cares and griefs are known only to thee, and from thee only came the cause.

"Cupid, why did thou wound me so deeply?"

"My mother told me to draw my arrow to the head," Cupid replied.

"Venus, why did thou prove so hateful?" Sappho asked.

"Cupid took a wrong shaft — a wrong arrow," Venus said.

Cupid had gold arrows and lead arrows. A person hit with a gold arrow feels love. A person hit with a lead arrow feels hate.

"Oh, Cupid, too unkind [cruel and unnatural], to make me so kind [so much in love], that I almost transgress the modesty of my kind [my gender]," Sappho said.

"I was blind, and I could not see my arrow," Cupid said.

"How did it come to pass that thou did hit my heart?" Sappho asked.

"That came by the nature of the head, which being once let out of the bow, can find no other alighting — landing — place but the heart," Cupid said.

"Don't be dismayed," Venus said. "Phao shall yield."

Sappho replied, "If he does yield, then I shall be ashamed to embrace one so mean and socially low; if he does not yield, I shall die, because I cannot embrace one so mean and cruel. Thus do I find no mean."

A mean is a middle ground. Sappho's two options each ended in an extreme: shame or her death.

"Well, I will work for thee and help thee," Venus said. "Farewell."

"Farewell, sweet Venus, and thou, Cupid, who are sweetest in thy sharpness," Sappho said.

Sappho exited.

Venus and Cupid talked together in Sappho's bedchamber.

"Cupid, what have thou done?" Venus asked. "Put thine arrows in Phao's eyes, and wounded thy mother's heart?"

"You gave him a face to allure, so then why shouldn't I give him eyes to pierce?" Cupid replied.

A glance from Phao had caused Venus to fall in love with him. It was if Phao's eyes were shooting Cupid's gold arrows.

Venus said:

"Oh, Venus! Unhappy Venus! In bestowing a benefit upon a man, thou have brought a bane — a poison — to a goddess. What perplexities and bewilderment do thou feel?

"Oh, fair Phao! And therefore made fair to breed in me a frenzy!

"Oh, I wish that when I gave thee golden locks to curl thy head, I had shackled thee with iron locks on thy feet! And when I nursed thee, Sappho, with lettuce, I wish that it had turned to hemlock!"

Lettuce is an edible plant, and hemlock is a poisonous plant.

Venus continued:

"Have I brought a smooth skin over thy — Phao's — face, to make a rough scar in my heart?

Lettuce is a smooth plant, and hemlock is a rough plant.

Venus continued:

"And have I given thee a fresh color like the damask rose, to make mine pale like the stained turquoise?"

In this society, people believed that turquoise would turn lighter if the wearer was about to be in danger.

Venus continued:

"Oh, Cupid, thy flames with Psyche's were only sparks, and my desires with Adonis were only dreams, compared to these unfamiliar torments."

Venus was jealous of the mortal woman Psyche, and she sent Cupid to kill her, but Cupid fell in love with the mortal Psyche, and he made a home for her and slept with her on the condition that she never see his face. Curious, Psyche looked at his face by candlelight as he was sleeping, and some candlewax fell on him and burned him. He fled, and Psyche wandered the earth in search of him.

After being scratched by one of Cupid's arrows, Venus fell in love with the good-looking Adonis, and she ignored everything but him.

Both love affairs were passionate, but Venus' current love for Phao was more passionate.

Venus continued:

"Laugh, Juno! Venus is in love; but Juno shall not see with whom, lest she be in love."

Venus was worried that if Juno, with whom she had a rivalry, saw Phao, she would also fall in love with him.

During the Trojan War, Venus supported the Trojans, while Juno and Minerva supported the Greeks. Earlier, the Trojan prince Paris had chosen Venus as the most beautiful goddess, with Juno and Minerva as runners-up.

Venus continued:

"Venus likely has become stale."

The word "stale" sometimes means "prostitute."

Venus continued:

"Sappho, indeed, because she has many virtues, she must therefore have all the favors. Venus grows old, and then she was a pretty wench, when Juno was a young wife; now a crow's foot is on her eye, and the black ox has trod on her foot.

Venus was growing older. She had laugh lines (crows' feet), and her feet hurt.

Venus continued:

"But were Sappho never so virtuous, does she think to contend with and compete against Venus and try to be as amorous?

"Yield, Phao; but yield to me, Phao.

"I entreat where I may command; thou command where thou should entreat."

Venus was an immortal goddess; Phao was a mere mortal man. Venus should be doing the commanding, according to Venus.

Venus continued:

"In this case, Cupid, what is thy counsel? Venus must both play the lover and the dissembler, and therefore the dissembler, because the lover."

According to Venus, lovers always dissemble.

Cupid said:

"You will forever be playing with arrows, like children with knives, and then, when you bleed, you cry."

He then gave his mother this advice:

"Go to Vulcan, entreat him with prayers, threaten him with blows, woo him with kisses, ban him with curses, and try all means to rid yourself of these extremities — this serious problem."

"To what end?" Venus asked. "Why should I do that?"

Cupid answered:

"So that he might make me new arrows, for nothing can root out the desires of Phao, but a new arrow of inconstancy and fickleness; nor can anything turn Sappho's heart away from loving Phao, except a new arrow of disdain.

Cupid would shoot Phao with a gold arrow to make him fall in love with someone other than Sappho, and he would shoot Sappho with a lead arrow to make her not love him.

Cupid continued:

"And then, they disliking one the other, who shall enjoy Phao but Venus?"

Venus said:

"I will follow thy counsel. For Venus, although she is in her latter age for years — she is old — yet she is in her nonage — her youth — for affections.

"When Venus ceases to love, let Jove cease to rule.

"But come, let us go to Vulcan."

Sappho, Mileta, Ismena, Eugenua, Lamia, Favilla, and Canope were in Sappho's bedchamber. They were discussing women's dreams.

Sappho said:

"What dreams are these, Mileta? And can there be no truth in dreams? Yes, dreams have their truth.

"I thought I saw a stockdove [wild pigeon] or woodquist [ringdove or wood pigeon], I don't know what to term it, that brought short straws to build his nest in a tall cedar, where, while with his bill he was framing his building — that is, building his nest — he lost as many feathers from his wings as he laid straws in his nest. Yet scrambling and struggling to catch hold to harbor and shelter in the house — that is, the nest — he had made, he suddenly fell from the bough where he stood.

"And then, pitifully casting up his eyes, he cried in such terms (as I imagined) as might either condemn the nature of such a tree, or the daring of such a mind."

The bird could condemn the tree for being so high, or it could condemn itself for attempting to build its nest so high.

In this allegory, of course, Phao is the bird, and Sappho is the tree.

Sappho continued:

"While he lay quaking upon the ground, and I was gazing on the cedar, I was able to see ants breed in the bark, coveting only to hoard food, and caterpillars to cleave and attach themselves to the leaves, laboring only to suck the leaves dry, which caused more leaves to fall from the tree, than there did feathers before from the dove."

The ants and caterpillars are parasites, literally and metaphorically.

Sappho continued:

"I thought, Mileta, that I sighed in my sleep, pitying both the fortune — luck, which was bad — of the bird, and the misfortune of the tree; but in this time, quills — that is, feathers — began to bud again in the bird, which made him look as though he would fly up, and then I wished that the body of the tree would bow down, so that he might just climb and creep up the tree.

"Then — and so —"

Sappho sighed.

"And so what?" Mileta asked.

Sappho said:

"Nothing Mileta, except — and so I waked.

"But did nobody dream but I?"

Mileta said:

"I dreamed last night — but I hope dreams are contrary."

She hoped that dreams did not forecast the future, but instead forecast the opposite of the future. Her dream was bad, and she hoped that it would not come true.

Mileta continued:

"While I was holding my head over a sweet smoke, all my hair blazed on a bright flame. I thought Ismena threw water to quench it, yet the sparks fell on my bosom, and, wiping them away with my hand, I was all covered in gory blood, until someone with a few fresh flowers staunched it and stopped the flow of blood.

"And so stretching myself because I was stiff, I startled and woke up: It was only a dream."

Ismena interpreted the dream: "It is a sign you shall fall in love after hearing fair words spoken by the one you will love. Water signifies counsel and advice, flowers signify death, and nothing can purge your loving humor but death."

Mileta had fallen in love with Phao, who was handsome, but he was also clumsy with words.

Mileta said, "You are no interpreter, but an inter-prater, harping always upon love, until you are as blind as a harper."

An inter-prater prates and chatters at intervals.

Ismena related her own dream: "I remember two nights ago: I dreamed my eyetooth — my canine tooth — was loose, and that I thrust it out with my tongue."

Mileta interpreted the dream: "It foretells the loss of a friend: and I always thought thee so full of prattling idle talk, that thou would thrust out thy best friend with thy tattling."

The loss of a friend? Which friend? Mileta.

Ismena said, "Yes, Mileta, but it was loose before; and if my friend is loose, it is as good to thrust out my friend with plain words, as to keep the friendship with dissembling."

A loose friend is a wanton friend. Ismena believed that it was better to break up a friendship with a loose friend than to continue a false friendship.

That friendship was with Mileta.

Eugenua gave her opinion about dreams: "Dreams are just foolishness, which are brought on either by things we see in the day, or some kinds of food that we eat, and so the common sense promotes it to be the imaginative."

Sappho thought that dreams may be true.

Mileta hoped that dreams are false.

Eugenua thought that dreams are brought on by indigestion or the imagination.

Ismena objected: "Wait a moment, philosophatrix, well skilled in the secrets of the art and science, and not seduced and misled by the superstitions of nature!"

A philosophatrix is a woman philosopher.

A meretrix is a prostitute, so a philosophatrix may be a philosophical prostitute — or a wanton friend putting on intellectual airs.

Some hurtful insults were being said among the court ladies.

Sappho said:

"Ismena's tongue never lies still. I think all her teeth will be loose, they are so often jogged against her tongue.

"But talk on, Eugenua."

"That is all I have to say," Eugenua said.

"What did you dream, Canope?" Sappho asked.

Canope said:

"I seldom dream, madam, but ever since your sickness, I cannot tell whether with being exhausted from watching over you, but I have had many fantastical visions; for even now, slumbering by your bed's side, I thought I was shadowed with and enclosed in a cloud, where laboring to unwrap myself, I was more entangled. But in the midst of my striving, it seemed to mizzle — drizzle — gold, with fair drops. I filled my lap, and as I ran to show the gold to my fellows, it turned to dust.

"I blushed, they laughed, and then I woke up, glad it was only a dream."

"Take heed, Canope, that gold does not tempt your lap, and then you blush for shame," Ismene said.

In other words: Beware, Canope. Don't fall for a man just because he showers you with gifts.

In a myth, Jupiter came to Danae in a shower of gold and impregnated her. She gave birth to the hero Perseus.

"It is good luck to dream of gold," Canope said.

"Yes, if it had continued to be gold when you woke up," Ismene said.

Lamia said:

"I dream every night, and last night I dreamed this:

"I thought that, walking in the sun, I was stung with the tarantula fly, whose venom nothing can expel but the sweet consent — the sweet harmony — of music. I tried all kinds of instruments, but found no ease and release from the bite, until, at the last, two lutes tuned in one key so glutted my thirsting ears that my grief presently ceased, for joy whereof as I was clapping my hands, your ladyship called."

Mileta interpreted the dream:

"It is a sign that nothing shall alleviate your love except marriage, for such is the tying of two in wedlock as is the tuning of two lutes in one key.

"For striking the strings of the one, straws will stir upon the strings of the other; just as in two minds linked in love, one cannot be delighted unless the other rejoices."

When two lutes are tuned in the same key, playing one lute's strings will cause the other lute's strings to gently vibrate like a soft wind causing a straw to gently move. These are sympathetic vibrations.

Sometimes, a man and a woman make beautiful music together.

Favilla related a dream:

"I thought, going by the seaside among pebbles, I saw someone playing with a round stone, always throwing it into the water when the sun shined.

"I asked what the name of the stone was, and he said it was called 'asbeston,' which, being once hot, would never be cold."

He had been throwing the asbeston stone into the sea to keep it cool when the sun shined.

Favilla continued relating her dream:

"He gave it to me and vanished.

"I, forgetting myself, delighted with the pretty show of the stone, would always show it by candlelight, pull it out in the sun, and see how bright it would look in the fire, where, catching heat, nothing could cool it.

"Out of anger, I threw it against the wall, and, with the heaving up of my arm, I awakened."

Mileta said, "Beware of love, Favilla; for women's hearts are such stones that, when warmed by affection, they cannot be cooled by wisdom."

"I assure you that I beware of love, for I never believe men's words," Favilla replied.

"Yet be wary, for women are scorched sometimes with men's eyes, although they had rather consume than confess," Ismena said.

Men would rather pine and waste away than admit that they are in love.

Sappho said:

"Cease your talking; for I would like to sleep, to see if I can dream whether the bird has feathers or ants have wings."

She wanted to see if she could continue the dream that she had related earlier.

She then said:

"Draw the curtain."

The court ladies closed the curtain.

— 4.4 —

Venus and Cupid entered Vulcan's forge, where Vulcan and Calypho were working.

Vulcan's forge was his workshop where, assisted by the one-eyed Cyclopes, he forged Jupiter's thunderbolts. The forge was located under Mount Etna, a volcano in Sicily.

Venus was here to request a favor from Vulcan, her husband. She wanted him to make new arrows for Cupid, her son.

Vulcan was often suspicious of Venus and her motives.

Vulcan is Venus' husband.

Cupid is Venus' son.

Was Vulcan Cupid's father?

Nope.

Who was Cupid's father?

Maybe Mars.

Maybe Mercury.

Maybe Jupiter.

Venus got around.

Vulcan had reason to be suspicious of Venus and her motives.

Venus said:

"Come, Cupid, Vulcan's flames must quench Venus' fires — her passion."

She called, "Vulcan?"

Vulcan looked up.

"Who is it?" he asked.

Venus answered, "Venus."

"Ho! Ho!" Vulcan said. "Venus."

Venus said:

"Come, sweet Vulcan. Thou know how sweet thou have found Venus, who, being of all the goddesses the most fair and beautiful, has chosen thee, of all the gods the most foul and ugliest, to be her spouse."

Earlier, she had said that her husband was chosen for her by lot.

Venus continued:

"Thou must necessarily then confess that I was most loving.

76

"Don't inquire about the reason for my request by questions but prevent the effects — anticipate the results — by courtesy.

"Make for me six arrowheads. It is given thee of the gods by permission to frame them to any purpose for which I shall request them by prayer."

Vulcan could give the arrowheads whatever power he — or his wife — wanted them to have.

Vulcan looked unhappy at this request.

Venus continued:

"Why do thou scowl and frown, Vulcan? Will thou have a kiss? Hold up thy head: Venus has young thoughts and fresh affections."

She kissed him and then said:

"Roots have strings [root filaments], when boughs have no leaves."

Venus' marriage had roots, while her affairs had no leaves.

Roots stay alive in the winter while all the leaves are dead.

Even when the marriage of Venus and Vulcan was frosty, it was still alive: There was something there.

Venus continued:

"But listen in thine ear, Vulcan."

She whispered something to him and then asked:

"What do thou say?"

Vulcan replied:

"Vulcan is a god with you when you are disposed to flatter.

"You are a true woman, whose tongue is like a bee's sting, which pricks deepest when it is fullest of honey."

Venus was at her most dangerous and her most deceptive when she flattered.

Vulcan continued:

"Because you have made my eyes drunk with beautiful looks, you will set my ears on edge with sweet words.

"You were accustomed to say that the beating of hammers made your head ache, and the smoke of the forge made your eyes water, and every coal was a block in your way.

"You weep rose water when you ask, and spit vinegar when you have obtained what you want.

"What do you want now with new arrows? Perhaps Mars has a tougher skin on his heart, or Cupid has a weaker arm, or Venus has a better courage."

Perhaps Venus had a new conquest in sight.

Vulcan continued:

"Well, Venus, there is never a smile in your face but has made a wrinkle in my forehead."

The wrinkles may be caused by worry, or by the horns of a cuckold, or by both.

Vulcan continued:

"Ganymede must fill your cup, and you will pledge and drink a toast to no one but Jupiter."

Ganymede was the cupbearer to the gods: He filled wine glasses.

Venus wanted the best: She wanted a luxurious life.

Vulcan concluded:

"But I will not chide Venus."

He did not want to argue with her.

Vulcan then said to Calypho:

"Come, Cyclops, my wife must have her will.

"Let us do that on earth which the gods cannot undo in heaven."

"That" means "make someone fall in love."

Venus replied:

"Gramercy, sweet Vulcan. Thank you.

"Get to your work."

As Vulcan made the arrows, he sang:

"My shag-hair Cyclops, come let's ply

"Our Lemnian hammers lustily [vigorously].

"By my wife's sparrows,

"I swear these arrows

"Shall singing fly

"Through many a wanton's eye.

"These headed are with golden blisses,

"These silver ones [are] feathered with kisses,

"But this of lead

"Strikes a clown [rustic, fool] dead,

"When in a dance

"He falls in a trance.

"To see his black-brow lass not buss [kiss] him,

"And then whines out for

"Death t' untruss [to release] him.

"So, so, our work being done, let's play,

"Holiday, boys, cry holiday!"

"Lemnian" refers to the island of Lemnos.

Usually, Vulcan's lead arrows make someone hate another person, but according to the song, these lead arrows make the person whose heart they enter fall down and whine that he wants to be dead because the person he loves does not love him.

Silver arrows? In classical mythology, Cupid had only gold and lead arrows.

Vulcan said, "Here, Venus, I have finished these arrows by art and skill, and I bestow them to you by wit and intelligence; for he must use as great advice — prudence — who has them, as he who made them used cunning."

"Vulcan, now you have done with your forge, don't tell us about your flights of fancy," Venus said. "You are the fletcher — the maker — of the arrows; you are not the archer. You should meddle with the arrow, not the aim."

Before, Venus had been sweet, but now she had what she wanted. She had dissembled to get what she wanted.

Vulcan said:

"I thought so: When I have done working, you have done wooing. Where is now 'sweet Vulcan'?

"Well, I can say no more but this, which is enough and as much as any can say: Venus is a woman."

"Don't be angry, Vulcan," Venus said. "I will love thee again, when I have either business or nothing else to do."

"When I have business" means "When I want something."

"Nothing else to do" means "When I haven't found someone better than you."

Cupid said, "My mother will make much of you, when there are no more men than Vulcan."

According to Cupid, Venus would make much of Vulcan when Vulcan was the last man on earth.

Vulcan went deeper into his forge. He was out of hearing distance.

CHAPTER 5

— 5.1 —

Venus and Cupid talked together in Vulcan's forge.

Venus said:

"Come, Cupid, receive with thy step-father's instruments — the six arrows — thy mother's instructions, for thou must be wise in judgment, if thou will be fortunate in execution."

Venus described **Arrow #1** — Arrowhead of the Stone Perillus:

"This arrow is feathered with the wings of aegitus, which never sleeps for jealous fear of his hen."

The aegitus was a hawk that was lame: Venus described it as being jealous of its mate.

Vulcan was also lame and jealous of his wife.

Venus continued:

"The head is touched with the stone perillus, which causes mistrust and jealousy.

"Shoot this, Cupid, at men who have beautiful wives who will make them rub the brows when they swell in the brains."

They will rub their brows to see whether cuckold's horns are growing because their brains are swelling with jealous thoughts.

Venus described **Arrow #2** — Arrowhead of Lydian Steel:

"This shaft is headed with Lydian steel, which strikes the heart and induces a deep disdain of that which we most desire; the feathers are of turtledoves, but they are dipped in the blood of a tigress.

"Draw this up close to the head at Sappho, so that the arrow may hit her with great force and she may despise where now she dotes.

"My good boy, wound her in the side, so that for Phao's love she may never sigh."

Venus described **Arrow #3** — Arrowhead of the Eagle's Beak:

"This arrow is feathered with the phoenix' wing, and it is headed with the eagle's beak."

The phoenix is a mythological bird that lives for 500 years, sets itself on fire, and rises newly born from the ashes.

Venus continued:

"It makes men passionate in desires, constant and loyal in love, and wise in conveyance [courtship], melting, as it were, their fancies into faith.

"This arrow, sweet child, and with as great aim as thou can, Phao must be stricken with. Cry softly to thyself in the very release of the arrow, 'Venus!'

"Sweet Cupid, don't mistake what I say and don't make a mistake. I will make a quiver for that by itself."

Venus described **Arrow #4** — Arrowhead of Fine Gold:

"The fourth has feathers of the peacock, but they are glued with the gum of the myrtle tree, headed with fine gold, and the gold arrowhead is fastened to the shaft with brittle chrysocolla, a glue.

"Shoot this arrow at dainty and coy ladies, at amiable, lovely, and young nymphs.

"Choose no other white" — think of the white center of a target — "except women, for this will work liking in their minds, but not love; affability and geniality in speech, but no faith, no loyalty, and no constancy; courtly favors to be mistresses over many, but constant to none; sighs to be fetched from the lungs, not the heart; and tears to be wrung out with their fingernails, not their eyes; secret laughing at men's pale looks and neat attire; open rejoicing at their own comeliness and beauty and at men's courting."

Tears wrung out with fingernails are caused by scratches.

Venus continued:

"Shoot this arrow among the thickest of them, whose bosoms lie open because they would be stricken with it. And seeing men term women 'Jupiter's fools,' women shall make men 'Venus' fools.'"

Women are Jupiter's fools because Jupiter has slept with so many mortal women.

Men shall be Venus' fools because women will string men along by flirting with them without being in love with them.

Venus described **Arrow #5** — Arrowhead of Lead:

"This shaft is lead in the head, and its black feathers are of the night raven: It is a deadly and poisoned shaft, which breeds nothing but hate against those who plead for love.

"Take heed, Cupid, that thou do not hit Phao with this arrow, for then shall Venus perish."

If Cupid were to hit Phao with this arrow, he would hate any woman or goddess who pursued him, including Venus.

Venus described **Arrow #6**:

"This last is an old arrow, just recently mended. It is the arrow that hit both Sappho and Phao, working only in mean minds an aspiring to superiors, and in high estates a stooping to inferiors.

"With this arrow, Cupid, I am galled — distressed — myself, until thou have galled — wounded — Phao with the other arrow: the one that brings faithful and constant love."

The arrow that brings faithful and constant love is **Arrow #3**: Arrowhead of the Eagle's Beak

Venus has been hit with **Arrow #6**: She was a goddess who has fallen in love with a lowly mortal man.

Cupid said, "I assure you that I will cause Phao to languish in your love and pine for you, and Sappho to disdain his love."

Venus said:

"Go. Don't loiter but instead make haste, and don't mistake your shaft. Be sure to hit the right person with the right arrow."

Interesting. Men are capable of true love (**Arrow #3**), while women are capable of liking (**Arrow #4**).

Cupid exited.

Venus continued:

"Now, Venus, thou have played a cunning part, although not current."

"Not current" meant not ethical.

Venus continued:

"But why should Venus dispute about unlawfulness in love, or faith in affection, as Venus is both the goddess of love and affection and she knows that there is as little truth to be used in love, as there is reason?

"No, sweet Phao, Venus will obtain and possess thee because she is Venus. Not thou, Jove, with thunder in thy hand, shall take him out of my hands. I have new arrows now for my boy, and fresh flames at which the gods shall tremble, if they begin to trouble me.

"But I will wait for the outcome of my instructions to Cupid, and I will wait for Cupid at the forge of my husband."

— 5.2 —

Sappho, Cupid, and Mileta talked together in a room in Sappho's palace.

"What have thou done, Cupid?" Sappho asked.

"I have done what my mother commanded, Sappho," Cupid answered.

"I think I feel an alteration in my mind, and, as it were, a withdrawing into myself of my own affections and lovesickness," Sappho said.

"Then my arrow has had its effect," Cupid said.

Cupid had shot her with **Arrow #2**: the arrow that caused the recipient to dislike whomever she had previously liked.

"I ask thee to please tell me the reason you shot me with one of your arrows," Sappho said.

"I dare not," Cupid said.

Sappho said:

"Fear nothing, for if Venus frets and complains, Sappho can frown.

"Thou shall be my son.

"Mileta, give him some sweetmeats."

Mileta did.

Sweetmeats are sweet food such as cakes and sugared nuts and candied fruits.

Sappho continued:

"Speak, good Cupid, and I will give thee many pretty things."

"My mother is in love with Phao," Cupid said. "She wanted me to strike you with disdain of him, and to strike him with desire of her."

Sappho said:

"Oh, spiteful Venus!

"Mileta, give him some of that."

Mileta gave Cupid more sweetmeats.

Sappho then asked:

"What else, Cupid?"

Cupid said, "I could get even with my mother, and so I will if I may call you mother."

"Yes, Cupid, call me anything, as long as I may get even with her," Sappho said.

"I have an arrow, with which if I strike Phao, it will cause him to loathe only Venus," Cupid said.

Only Venus currently loved Phao, and the arrow would cause Phao to loathe only those who currently loved him.

The arrow is **Arrow #5**: the lead arrow.

"Sweet Cupid, strike Phao with it," Sappho said. "Thou shall sit in my lap: I will rock thee asleep and feed thee with all these fine knacks — these fine delicacies."

"I will set about doing it," Cupid said.

He exited.

Sappho said after him:

"But come quickly again."

She then said to herself:

"Ah, unkind Venus, is this thy promise to Sappho?"

Earlier, Venus had promised to help her. This was not the kind of "help" Sappho wanted.

Sappho continued:

"But if I get Cupid from thee, I myself will be the queen of love. I will direct these arrows with better aim, and I will conquer my own affections with greater modesty. Venus' heart shall flame, and her love shall be as common, indiscriminate, and sluttish as her craft."

Sappho will use the arrows to make herself be in control of her emotions, but also to make Venus always passionately in love.

Venus' craft is deceit.

Sappho then said:

"Oh, Mileta, time has disclosed that which my temperance and self-control have kept hidden and in secret; but since I am rid of the disease, I will not be ashamed to confess the cause."

Her disease was lovesickness, and the cause was her love for Phao.

Sappho continued:

"I loved Phao, Mileta, a thing unfit for my social rank, but forced by my desire."

"Phao?" Mileta asked.

"Phao, Mileta, of whom now Venus is enamored," Sappho answered.

"And do you love him still?" Mileta asked.

Sappho said:

"No, I feel my love thoughts abating, and I feel my reason not yielding to appetite.

"Let Venus have him — no, she shall not have him.

"But here comes Cupid."

Cupid entered the scene and sat on Sappho's lap.

She asked, "How are things now, my boy? Have thou done it?"

Cupid said, "Yes, and I have left Phao ranting against Venus, and cursing her name; yet still sighing for Sappho, and emblazening and proclaiming her virtues."

Phao had been hit with **Arrow #5**, which caused him to hate those who were pursuing him. That person was the goddess Venus. Since Sappho no longer loved Phao, **Arrow #5** did not cause him to hate her. Instead, he continued to love her.

Sappho said:

"Alas, poor Phao! Thy extreme love should not be requited with so mean a fortune; thy fair face deserved greater favors. I cannot love you: Venus has hardened my heart."

Sappho was sympathetic to Phao. **Arrow #2** had not caused Sappho to dislike him, but only to not love him.

Venus entered the scene.

She said to herself:

"I marvel Cupid has not come all this while."

She had grown tired of waiting for him, and so she had come looking for him.

Seeing him and Sappho, she said:

"What is this now? Why are thou sitting in Sappho's lap?"

"Yes, Venus, what do you say about it?" Sappho said. "Cupid is sitting in Sappho's lap."

"Sir boy, come here," Venus said.

"I will not," Cupid responded.

"What is this now?" Venus said. "You will not! Has Sappho made you so saucy?

"I will be Sappho's son," Cupid said. "I have, as you commanded, strickened her with a deep disdain of Phao; and I have stricken Phao, as Sappho entreated and asked me, with a great hatred of you."

"Unhappy wag — trouble-causing boy — what have thou done?" Venus said. "I will make thee repent it in every vein of thy heart."

Sappho said:

"Venus, don't be choleric and angry.

"Cupid is mine. He has given me his arrows, and I will give him a new bow to shoot arrows with.

"You are not worthy to be the lady of love, you who yield so often to the deep impressions of love. You are immodest, Venus, who, to satisfy the unbridled and uncontrolled thoughts of thy heart, have transgressed so far from the restraint of thine honor.

"What do thou say, Cupid? Will thou stay with me?"

"Yes," Cupid said.

"Won't I be on earth the goddess of affections?" Sappho asked.

"Yes," Cupid said.

"Won't I rule the fancies of men, and figuratively lead Venus in chains like a captive?"

Sappho planned to make Venus fall repeatedly in love.

"Yes," Cupid said.

"It is a good boy!" Sappho said.

Venus said:

"What have we here? You the goddess of love?

"And you her son, Cupid?

"I will tame that proud heart of Sappho's, or else the gods shall say that they are not Venus' friends.

"And as for you, sir boy, I will teach you how to run away.

"You shall be stripped from top to toe, and whipped with nettles, not roses. I will set you to blow Vulcan's coals, not to bear Venus' quiver. I will deal with you because of this matter.

"Well, I will say no more, although there is more that I could say.

"But as for the new mistress of love (or, lady, I beg your mercy, I think you would rather be called a goddess), you shall know what it is to usurp the name of Venus!

"I will pull those plumes and cause you to cast your eyes on your feet, not your feathers."

Peacock feathers are lovely, but peacock feet are ugly.

Venus continued:

"I will turn your soft hair to hard bristles, your tongue to a sting, and those alluring eyes to eyes unlucky in luring men, in which, if the gods do not aid me, I will curse the gods!"

Sappho said:

"Venus, you are in a vein — a mood — answerable to your vanity, whose high and haughty words of outrage neither become you, nor frighten me.

"But let this suffice: I will keep Cupid in spite of you, and yet with the content and consent of the gods."

Venus said:

"Will you? Why then, we shall have 'pretty' gods in heaven, when you take gods prisoners on earth. Before I sleep, you shall both repent, and you shall find what it is merely to think irreverently and disrespectfully of Venus.

"Come, Cupid. She does not know how to treat and employ thee. Come with me. You know what I have for you.

"Won't you come with me?"

According to what Venus had said earlier, she had a beating with nettles in store for him.

"Not I!" Cupid said.

"Well, I will be even with you both, and that shortly," Venus said.

Venus exited.

"Cupid, don't be afraid," Sappho said. "I will direct thine arrows better. Every rude ass shall not say he is in love. It is a toy made for ladies, and I will keep it only for ladies."

"But what will you do for Phao?" Cupid asked.

Sappho said:

"I will wish him fortunate — I will wish him good luck. This I will do for Phao because I once loved Phao. For never shall it be said that Sappho loved to hate, or that out of love she could not be as courteous as she was in love passionate.

"Come, Mileta, shut the door."

They exited.

— 5.3 —

Phao stood in front of Sybilla's cave.

He said to himself:

"Go to Sybilla. Tell her the beginning of thy love, and the end of thy good fortune.

"And look! Luckily, she sits in her cave."

He called:

"Sybilla!"

"Phao, welcome," Sybilla said. "What is the news?"

Phao replied:

"I loathe Venus, the goddess of love.

"Cupid caused it with a new shaft: He shot me with a new arrow.

"Sappho disdains me.

"Venus caused it because of a newly formed spite.

"Oh, Sybilla, if even Venus is unfaithful in love, where shall one fly for truth and faithfulness? She uses deceit, so isn't it then likely she will permit subtlety and cunning? And being careful to commit injuries, won't she not care whom she hurts to revenge them?"

In other words: Venus takes great care to commit injuries, and she will be eager to revenge them, not caring whom she hurts in the process.

Phao continued:

"I must now fall from love to labor, and endeavor with my oar to get a fare, not with my pen to write a fancy: a love sonnet.

"Loves are only illusory smokes, which vanish in the seeing and yet hurt while they are seen."

He paused and said to himself:

"A ferry, Phao?

"No, the stars cannot call it a worser fortune."

Being a ferryman was not a worser fortune: Phao had previously been happy as a ferryman.

Being deprived of Sappho was a worser fortune.

Phao added:

"Wander rather over the world, swear off affections, and beg for death."

Phao then said:

"Oh, Sappho, thou have Cupid in thine arms; I have him in my heart.

"Thou kiss him for sport and entertainment; I must curse him for spite.

"Yet I will not curse him, Sappho, whom thou kiss.

"This shall be my resolution:

"Wherever I wander, I resolve to be as if I were always kneeling before Sappho, my loyalty unspotted and undiminished, although unrewarded.

"I will go to my grave with as little malice as I did lie with in my cradle. My life shall be spent in sighing and wishing, the one for my bad fortune, the other for Sappho's good fortune."

Sybilla said:

"Do so, Phao, for destiny calls thee as well from Sicily as from love.

"Other things hang over thy head, which I must neither tell, nor thou inquire.

"And so, farewell."

Sybilla exited.

Alone, Phao said:

"Farewell, Sybilla, and farewell, Sicily."

About himself, he said:

"Thoughts shall be thy food, and in thy steps shall be imprinted behind thee that there was none as loyal left behind thee.

"Farewell, Syracuse, which is unworthy to harbor faith; and when I am gone, unless Sappho is here, it is unlikely to harbor any."

Phao exited.

EPILOGUE

The Epilogue appeared and said:

"They who tread in a maze, walk often in one path, and at the last come out where they entered in.

"We fear we have led you all this while in a labyrinth of trifles, several times hearing one idea, and we have now brought you to an end where we first began.

"This wearisome travail and travel you must impute to the necessity of the history, as Theseus did his labor to the art of the labyrinth."

Theseus entered the labyrinth of Crete at one place, and he exited at the same place, using a thread to find his way out.

The Epilogue continued:

"There is nothing that causes such giddiness and dizziness as going in a wheel. Neither can there be anything that breeds such tediousness as hearing many words uttered in a small area.

"But if you accept this dance of a fairy in a circle, we will hereafter at your wills frame our fingers to all forms.

"And so we wish every one of you a thread to lead you out of the doubts, wherewith we leave you entangled, so that nothing will be mistaken by our rash oversights, nor misconstrued by your deep insights."

The Epilogue hoped that the audience of the play would not overinterpret it and think it applied to such real people as, say, Queen Elizabeth I.

The Epilogue also apologized for leaving his characters in the same situation that they were in before his play began.

Phao, however, had changed from a happy man to an unhappy man.

NOTES

— 1.1 —

Below is the story about Venus and Mars being caught in a net by Vulcan. The story is told by the blind poet Demodocus in Homer's *Odyssey*. Of course, the *Odyssey* uses the Greek names of the gods. Venus is Aphrodite. Mars is Ares. Vulcan is Hephaestus. Mercury is Hermes. Jupiter is Zeus. Neptune is Poseidon.

Demodocus sang a comic song of Aphrodite's affair with Ares, the god of war. The two had fallen in lust although Aphrodite, the goddess of sexual passion, was married to Hephaestus, the gifted blacksmith god. Hephaestus learned of the affair, so he set a trap for the illicit lovers. He created fine chains that bound tightly, he placed the chains above his bed, and then he pretended to leave his mansion to journey abroad. Ares ran to Aphrodite and invited her to join him in Hephaestus' bed, and together they ran to the bed. Ares and Aphrodite lay down in bed together, and then the fine chains snared them, locked in lust.

Hephaestus returned home, knowing what and whom he would see in his bed. He invited all the gods and the goddesses to look, also. He complained to Zeus, "Father, look at how my wife treats me. I am crippled, so she sleeps with Ares because of his handsome looks. Right now, they are in my bed, locked together in the act of lovemaking by chains that only I can loosen. Come, look and laugh at the lovers. I will keep them bound until I receive my bride-gifts back. The goddess I married is a bitch."

The gods entered Hephaestus' bedroom and looked at the unhappy and embarrassed Ares and Aphrodite, naked and stuck together. The goddesses, however, were embarrassed and stayed away.

The gods laughed, and one god said to another, "Hephaestus one, adulterers zero. The blacksmith god conquers both the god of war and the goddess of sexual passion."

Apollo asked Hermes, "Would bedding Aphrodite be worth the embarrassment of being caught by Hephaestus?"

Hermes replied, "Of course! Look how beautiful she is!"

Only Poseidon did not laugh; he was a friend to Ares. He begged Hephaestus to release the lovers, saying, "Ares will pay you whatever you ask for sleeping with your wife."

Hephaestus replied, "Ares is a worthless god, and a promise from a worthless god is a worthless promise, so don't ask me to release him from my chains."

But Poseidon said, "If he won't pay the fine, I will. My word is good."

"So it is," Hephaestus said. He released the two lovers, who ran away in opposite directions to friends who would not laugh at them.

Source of Above: David Bruce, *Homer's* Odyssey: *A Retelling in Prose.*
https://www.smashwords.com/books/view/87553

— 1.1 —

Mithridate is an antidote for poison. The name derives from Mithridates.

This is the end of A.E. Housman's poem "Terence, This is Stupid Stuff," from his book *A Shropshire Lad*:

There was a king reigned in the East:
There, when kings will sit to feast,
They get their fill before they think
With poisoned meat and poisoned drink.
He gathered all that sprang to birth
From the many-venomed earth;
First a little, thence to more,
He sampled all her killing store;
And easy, smiling, seasoned sound,
Sate the king when healths went round.
They put arsenic in his meat
And stared aghast to watch him eat;
They poured strychnine in his cup
And shook to see him drink it up:
They shook, they stared as white's their shirt:
Them it was their poison hurt.
— I tell the tale that I heard told.
Mithridates, he died old.

— 3.4 —

For Your Information:

The combining form -phage is used like a suffix meaning "a thing that devours." It is used in many scientific terms, especially in biology.

The form -phage ultimately comes from the Greek phageîn, meaning "to eat, devour." This Greek root also helps form the word esophagus. [...] The word phage, referring to a bacteriophage, is a shortened or independent use of the combining form -phage.

Closely related to -phage are -plagia, -phagy, and -phagous. Their corresponding form combined to the beginning of words is phago-.

Source of Above:
"-phagous." Dictionary.com. Accessed 6 October 2022.
https://www.dictionary.com/browse/-phage

— 3.4 —

For Your Information:

> *The tortoise was the symbol of the ancient Greek city of Aegina, on the island by the same name: the seal and coins of the city shows images of tortoises. The word Chelonian comes from the Greek Chelone, a tortoise god. The tortoise was a fertility symbol in Greek and Roman times, and an attribute of Aphrodite/Venus.*

This is a photo caption in the Wikipedia article:

> *Aphrodite Ourania, draped rather than nude, and with her foot resting on a tortoise at Musée du Louvre.*

Source of Above:
"Cultural depictions of turtles." Wikipedia. Accessed 6 October 2022.
https://en.wikipedia.org/wiki/Cultural_depictions_of_turtles
For More Information:
Carol L. Dougherty: "Why Does Aphrodite Have Her Foot on That Turtle?"
Arion: A Journal of Humanities and the Classics
Vol. 27, No. 3 (Winter 2020), 25-48 (24 pages)pp.
https://www.jstor.org/stable/arion.27.3.0025
https://muse.jhu.edu/article/815705/pdf

95

$$— 3.4 —$$

The passage below is from my retelling of Apollonius of Rhodes' *Argonautica*:

They followed a path to the sacred wood where the Golden Fleece hung from a tree. The Golden Fleece was bright like a cloud that has been colored by the Sun at dawn. The huge snake that guarded the Golden Fleece with its never-sleeping eyes saw them and hissed at them. The hiss traveled a far distance, and it startled babies. Mothers held their babies closer and hugged them.

The snake came closer to Medea and Jason, but Medea began to chant, invoking the god of Sleep to come and overpower the snake. She also invoked the dreaded goddess Hecate. Jason, terrified, stood behind Medea. The snake, hearing Medea's words, began to relax its body, but its head swayed over Medea and Jason and threatened to swallow them.

Medea, still chanting, dipped some freshly cut juniper in a potion and sprinkled the snake's eyes with her magic. The eyes that had never slept before now slept. The snake's head and body lay on the ground, overcome by the scent of the magic potion. Following Medea's orders, Jason got the Golden Fleece from the tree while Medea continued to anoint the snake's head with her magic potion. Jason called to her that he had gotten the Golden Fleece, and she left the snake as it slept.

Source of Above:

Bruce, David. *Jason and the Argonauts: A Retelling in Prose of Apollonius of Rhodes' Argonautica.* 2013.

https://www.smashwords.com/books/view/337653

— 4.4 —

Here is some information about the parentage of Eros, aka Cupid (bold added):

According to other genealogies, again, **Eros was a son of Hermes by Artemis or Aphrodite, or of Ares by Aphrodite** *(Cic. de Nat. Deor. iii. 23), or of Zephyrus and Iris (Plut. Amal. 20; Eustath. ad Hom.p. 555),* **or, lastly, a son of Zeus by his own daughter Aphrodite, so that Zeus was at once his father and grandfather.** *(Virg. Cir. 134.)*

Source of Above: "Eros." *Theoi.* Accessed 8 October 2022
https://www.theoi.com/Ouranios/Eros.html
Note: I don't understand this reference: *Virg. Cir. 134.*
Here is some more information:

Eros was a primeval god, son of Chaos, the original primeval emptiness of the universe, but later tradition made him the son of Aphrodite, goddess of sexual love and beauty, by either Zeus (the king of the gods), Ares (god of war and of battle), or Hermes (divine messenger of the gods).

Source of Above:
"Eros." Encyclopedia Britannica. 10 September 2022
https://www.britannica.com/topic/Eros-Greek-god

— Entire Play —

At times in this play, there appears to be forecasting that jealous people at the court will interfere with the love of Sappho and Phao. That does not happen. Instead, it is pride and different social classes, and the machinations of Venus and Cupid, that interfere with that love.

Phao's love does not change, but Sappho, whether in love or not with Phao, thinks that Phao is beneath her.

Phao is proud of his good looks, and he realizes that this is not good.

Sappho is proud of her birth, and she does not realize that such pride may not be good.

In 1.2, Trachinus talked about what could bring rottenness to Sappho's court: the east wind. In Genesis 41:6, the Pharoah dreamed of *"seven thin ears [of corn] blasted with the east wind"* (Bishop's Bible). In this play, the east wind is Venus and Cupid.

Prophets don't always see clearly, or prophets are not always understood properly. Instead of being wary of people at court, Phao needed to be wary of Venus and Cupid.

Sybilla was in part saying in her advice about how to act at court that if Phao continued to be sweet, innocent Phao, things would end badly for him.

Sappho's beauty and Phao's love were real. But Sappho's love was not real because she fell in love with Phao's good looks, which were not real because they were a gift from Venus.

Love does have power. Cupid's arrows are only partially effective. Cupid's **Arrow #2** should have made Sappho hate Phao, but she merely ceased to love him. She remembered that she had loved him.

APPENDIX A: FAIR USE

§ 107. Limitations on exclusive rights: Fair use
Release date: 2004-04-30

Notwithstanding the provisions of sections 106 and 106A, the fair use of a copyrighted work, including such use by reproduction in copies or phonorecords or by any other means specified by that section, for purposes such as criticism, comment, news reporting, teaching (including multiple copies for classroom use), scholarship, or research, is not an infringement of copyright. In determining whether the use made of a work in any particular case is a fair use the factors to be considered shall include —

(1) the purpose and character of the use, including whether such use is of a commercial nature or is for nonprofit educational purposes;

(2) the nature of the copyrighted work;

(3) the amount and substantiality of the portion used in relation to the copyrighted work as a whole; and

(4) the effect of the use upon the potential market for or value of the copyrighted work.

The fact that a work is unpublished shall not itself bar a finding of fair use if such finding is made upon consideration of all the above factors.

Source of Fair Use information:
http://www.law.cornell.edu/uscode/17/107.html

APPENDIX B: ABOUT THE AUTHOR

It was a dark and stormy night. Suddenly a cry rang out, and on a hot summer night in 1954, Josephine, wife of Carl Bruce, gave birth to a boy — me. Unfortunately, this young married couple allowed Reuben Saturday, Josephine's brother, to name their first-born. Reuben, aka "The Joker," decided that Bruce was a nice name, so he decided to name me Bruce Bruce. I have gone by my middle name — David — ever since.

Being named Bruce David Bruce hasn't been all bad. Bank tellers remember me very quickly, so I don't often have to show an ID. It can be fun in charades, also. When I was a counselor as a teenager at Camp Echoing Hills in Warsaw, Ohio, a fellow counselor gave the signs for "sounds like" and "two words," then she pointed to a bruise on her leg twice. Bruise Bruise? Oh yeah, Bruce Bruce is the answer!

Uncle Reuben, by the way, gave me a haircut when I was in kindergarten. He cut my hair short and shaved a small bald spot on the back of my head. My mother wouldn't let me go to school until the bald spot grew out again.

Of all my brothers and sisters (six in all), I am the only transplant to Athens, Ohio. I was born in Newark, Ohio, and have lived all around Southeastern Ohio. However, I moved to Athens to go to Ohio University and have never left.

At Ohio U, I never could make up my mind whether to major in English or Philosophy, so I got a bachelor's degree with a double major in both areas, then I added a Master of Arts degree in English and a Master of Arts degree in Philosophy. Yes, I have my MAMA degree.

Currently, and for a long time to come (I eat fruits and veggies), I am spending my retirement writing books such as *Nadia Comaneci: Perfect 10*, *The Funniest People in Comedy*, *Homer's* Iliad: *A Retelling in Prose*, and *William Shakespeare's* Hamlet: *A Retelling in Prose*.

If all goes well, I will publish one or two books a year for the rest of my life. (On the other hand, a good way to make God laugh is to tell Her your plans.)

By the way, my sister Brenda Kennedy writes romances such as *A New Beginning* and *Shattered Dreams*.

APPENDIX C: SOME BOOKS BY DAVID BRUCE

Retellings of a Classic Work of Literature

Ben Jonson's The Alchemist: *A Retelling*

Ben Jonson's The Arraignment, or Poetaster: *A Retelling*

Ben Jonson's Bartholomew Fair: *A Retelling*

Ben Jonson's The Case is Altered: *A Retelling*

Ben Jonson's Catiline's Conspiracy: *A Retelling*

Ben Jonson's The Devil is an Ass: *A Retelling*

Ben Jonson's Epicene: *A Retelling*

Ben Jonson's Every Man in His Humor: *A Retelling*

Ben Jonson's Every Man Out of His Humor: *A Retelling*

Ben Jonson's The Fountain of Self-Love, or Cynthia's Revels: *A Retelling*

Ben Jonson's The Magnetic Lady, or Humors Reconciled: *A Retelling*

Ben Jonson's The New Inn, or The Light Heart: *A Retelling*

Ben Jonson's Sejanus' Fall: *A Retelling*

Ben Jonson's The Staple of News: *A Retelling*

Ben Jonson's A Tale of a Tub: *A Retelling*

Ben Jonson's Volpone, or the Fox: *A Retelling*

Christopher Marlowe's Complete Plays: Retellings

Christopher Marlowe's Dido, Queen of Carthage: *A Retelling*

Christopher Marlowe's Doctor Faustus: *Retellings of the 1604 A-Text and of the 1616 B-Text*

Christopher Marlowe's Edward II: *A Retelling*

Christopher Marlowe's The Massacre at Paris: *A Retelling*

Christopher Marlowe's The Rich Jew of Malta: *A Retelling*

Christopher Marlowe's Tamburlaine, Parts 1 and 2: *Retellings*

Dante's Divine Comedy: *A Retelling in Prose*

Dante's Inferno: *A Retelling in Prose*

Dante's Purgatory: *A Retelling in Prose*

Dante's Paradise: *A Retelling in Prose*

The Famous Victories of Henry V: *A Retelling*

From the Iliad *to the* Odyssey: *A Retelling in Prose of Quintus of Smyrna's* Posthomerica

George Chapman, Ben Jonson, and John Marston's Eastward Ho! *A Retelling*

George Peele's The Arraignment of Paris: *A Retelling*

George Peele's The Battle of Alcazar: *A Retelling*

George Peele's David and Bathsheba, and the Tragedy of Absalom: *A Retelling*

George Peele's Edward I: *A Retelling*

George Peele's The Old Wives' Tale: *A Retelling*

George-a-Greene: *A Retelling*

The History of King Leir: *A Retelling*

Homer's Iliad: *A Retelling in Prose*

Homer's Odyssey: *A Retelling in Prose*

J.W. Gent.'s The Valiant Scot: *A Retelling*

Jason and the Argonauts: A Retelling in Prose of Apollonius of Rhodes' Argonautica

John Ford: Eight Plays Translated into Modern English

John Ford's The Broken Heart: *A Retelling*

John Ford's The Fancies, Chaste and Noble: *A Retelling*

John Ford's The Lady's Trial: *A Retelling*

John Ford's The Lover's Melancholy: *A Retelling*

John Ford's Love's Sacrifice: *A Retelling*

John Ford's Perkin Warbeck: *A Retelling*

John Ford's The Queen: *A Retelling*

John Ford's 'Tis Pity She's a Whore: *A Retelling*

John Lyly's Campaspe: *A Retelling*

John Lyly's Endymion, The Man in the Moon: *A Retelling*

John Lyly's Galatea: *A Retelling*

John Lyly's Love's Metamorphosis: *A Retelling*

John Lyly's Midas: *A Retelling*

John Lyly's Mother Bombie: *A Retelling*

John Lyly's Sappho and Phao: *A Retelling*

John Lyly's The Woman in the Moon: *A Retelling*

John Webster's The White Devil: *A Retelling*

King Edward III: *A Retelling*

Mankind: *A Medieval Morality Play* (A Retelling)

Margaret Cavendish's The Unnatural Tragedy: *A Retelling*

The Merry Devil of Edmonton: *A Retelling*

Robert Greene's Friar Bacon and Friar Bungay: *A Retelling*

The Taming of a Shrew: *A Retelling*

Tarlton's Jests: A Retelling

Thomas Middleton's A Chaste Maid in Cheapside: *A Retelling*

Thomas Middleton's Women Beware Women: *A Retelling*

Thomas Middleton and Thomas Dekker's The Roaring Girl: *A Retelling*

Thomas Middleton and William Rowley's The Changeling: *A Retelling*

The Trojan War and Its Aftermath: Four Ancient Epic Poems

Virgil's Aeneid: *A Retelling in Prose*

William Shakespeare's 5 Late Romances: Retellings in Prose

William Shakespeare's 10 Histories: Retellings in Prose

William Shakespeare's 11 Tragedies: Retellings in Prose

William Shakespeare's 12 Comedies: Retellings in Prose

William Shakespeare's 38 Plays: Retellings in Prose

William Shakespeare's 1 Henry IV, aka Henry IV, Part 1: *A Retelling in Prose*

William Shakespeare's 2 Henry IV, aka Henry IV, Part 2: *A Retelling in Prose*

William Shakespeare's 1 Henry VI, aka Henry VI, Part 1: *A Retelling in Prose*

William Shakespeare's 2 Henry VI, aka Henry VI, Part 2: *A Retelling in Prose*

William Shakespeare's 3 Henry VI, aka Henry VI, Part 3: *A Retelling in Prose*

William Shakespeare's All's Well that Ends Well: *A Retelling in Prose*

William Shakespeare's Antony and Cleopatra: *A Retelling in Prose*

William Shakespeare's As You Like It: *A Retelling in Prose*

William Shakespeare's The Comedy of Errors: *A Retelling in Prose*

William Shakespeare's Coriolanus: *A Retelling in Prose*

William Shakespeare's Cymbeline: *A Retelling in Prose*

William Shakespeare's Hamlet: *A Retelling in Prose*

William Shakespeare's Henry V: *A Retelling in Prose*

William Shakespeare's Henry VIII: *A Retelling in Prose*

William Shakespeare's Julius Caesar: *A Retelling in Prose*

William Shakespeare's King John: *A Retelling in Prose*

William Shakespeare's King Lear: *A Retelling in Prose*

William Shakespeare's Love's Labor's Lost: *A Retelling in Prose*

William Shakespeare's Macbeth: *A Retelling in Prose*

William Shakespeare's Measure for Measure: *A Retelling in Prose*

William Shakespeare's The Merchant of Venice: *A Retelling in Prose*

William Shakespeare's The Merry Wives of Windsor: *A Retelling in Prose*

William Shakespeare's A Midsummer Night's Dream: *A Retelling in Prose*

William Shakespeare's Much Ado About Nothing: *A Retelling in Prose*

William Shakespeare's Othello: *A Retelling in Prose*

William Shakespeare's Pericles, Prince of Tyre: *A Retelling in Prose*

William Shakespeare's Richard II: *A Retelling in Prose*

William Shakespeare's Richard III: *A Retelling in Prose*

William Shakespeare's Romeo and Juliet: *A Retelling in Prose*

William Shakespeare's The Taming of the Shrew: *A Retelling in Prose*

William Shakespeare's The Tempest: *A Retelling in Prose*

William Shakespeare's Timon of Athens: *A Retelling in Prose*

William Shakespeare's Titus Andronicus: *A Retelling in Prose*

William Shakespeare's Troilus and Cressida: *A Retelling in Prose*

William Shakespeare's Twelfth Night: *A Retelling in Prose*

William Shakespeare's The Two Gentlemen of Verona: *A Retelling in Prose*

William Shakespeare's The Two Noble Kinsmen: *A Retelling in Prose*

William Shakespeare's The Winter's Tale: *A Retelling in Prose*

www.ingramcontent.com/pod-product-compliance
Lightning Source LLC
Chambersburg PA
CBHW021232130726
47988CB00002B/928